K

C

told himself, betwee

He could either go o

attempt to play a part of which he did not know a single line; or he could venture into the night and fall foul of two Tolokovinite vampire hunters whose sole intentions were to destroy him. It did not take much longer than a second for Count Alucard to make up his mind.

BITE INTO THE VAMPIRE SERIES -
IT'S FANGTASTIC!

THE LAST VAMPIRE
THE VAMPIRE'S HOLIDAY
THE VAMPIRE'S REVENGE
THE VAMPIRE'S CHRISTMAS
THE VAMPIRE VANISHES
VAMPIRE PARK
THE VAMPIRE HUNT
VAMPIRE ISLAND

ILLUSTRATED BY
TONY ROSS

RED FOX

First published by The Bodley Head 1998
Red Fox edition 1999

Printed and bound in Great Britain by
Cox & Wyman Ltd, Reading, Berkshire

Papers used by Random House UK Limited
are natural, recyclable products made from wood grown in sustainable forests. The manufacturing processes conform to the environmental regulations of the country of origin.

RANDOM HOUSE UK Limited Reg. No. 954009

ISBN 0 09 965351 6

1

In the darkest dead of the Transylvanian night, Count Alucard, the last of the vampires, lay still and silent in his polished dark-wood coffin. His soft white shroud was pulled up snugly around his ears; his jet-black hair was nestling in the comfort of his lace-edged satin pillow.

"*Ah-whoo-OOOH-oooooh*!"

The distant howl of a lone wolf, prowling restlessly in the depths of the forest that stretched away beyond the ancient castle's moonlit walls, rose then faded on the warm night air. But the sound did not disturb the count. Count Alucard was fast asleep in his favourite deepest dungeon and the combined howling of the entire Tolokovin wolf-pack would not have disturbed his slumber.

Students of the Dracula legend may pause at this point to wonder what a real-live vampire was about, fast asleep while the moon was up? For, as anyone who knows anything at all on that subject will tell you, vampires are nocturnal creatures who spend their night-times cruising on dark membraneous widespread wing in search of their unfortunate victims – then take themselves to their coffins during daylight hours.

But although this may be true of most vampires, Count Alucard (whose name, as you may probably have guessed, spells "Dracula" backwards) is the exception. The count is unlike any other vampire who has ever lived. Count Alucard is a vegetarian vampire. The very thought of sinking his two needle-sharp pointy fangs into the neck of a human being is enough to make the count wrinkle up his nose and shiver with distaste. When Count Alucard is in need of food, there is nothing that can tempt his appetite more than a succulent ripe peach, a fresh sweet orange, or even half a kilo of firm, fleshy, deep purple plums. When he wants a drink, the count's favourite tipple is a tall glass of ice-tinkling tomato juice richly spiced with Worcester sauce.

"*Ah-whoo-OOOH-ooooh*!"

Again the lone wolf stretched out its neck, flattened its ears and howled into the night – this time closer to the castle. But still the count slept on.

Perhaps Count Alucard might not have slept quite so soundly had he known that, not too far away and during those same hours of darkness, three men had got together to scheme of a way to bring about his downfall. For although the count was a gentle creature who would not knowingly harm any living thing there was still sufficient ignorance and superstition in the world to make him often fear for his very life . . .

"What makes you think that it's genuine?" asked Henri Rumboll, the Mayor of Tolokovin, peering doubtfully at the wrinkled, crease-worn, ancient map which was spread out across the police station desk.

"What makes you think that it isn't?" growled Alphonse Kropotel, Tolokovin's police sergeant, his medals gleaming in the circle of golden light cast by the flickering oil-lamp.

"How did you come across it, Alphonse?" asked Eric Horowitz, the portly proprietor of Tolokovin's general grocery store.

"I've already told you," snapped the police sergeant. "I came across it quite by chance – it was hidden under the floorboards of an old gypsy woman's caravan I had cause to search a week or so ago."

"What would an old gypsy woman want with a map of Alucard Castle and the surrounding forest?" said the puzzled grocer.

"I've already explained that too," replied Sergeant Kropotel impatiently. "She didn't know that it was there. It could have lain concealed beneath that caravan's floorboards for years and years. Who knows? What's more – who *cares*?" Kropotel paused, glanced out of the police station window and up the mountainside to where Alucard Castle stood, pale and silvery in the moonlight. "All that matters to the three of us is that we now possess the means to put an end to that accursed demon of darkness who has plagued our lives for far too long."

"We will rouse every villager!" cried Henri Rumboll, nodding in agreement. "We will have them arm themselves with pitchforks, scythes and blazing torches – and then go up that mountain and storm the vampire's castle."

"We have been up there and stormed the castle a dozen times before," objected Eric Horowitz. "To what avail? The evil vampire has always found a means of managing to evade us."

"That was before we had the map, Horowitz!" snapped Sergeant Kropotel. "That castle is a rabbit warren of secret passages. This map shows every single one! We shall place guards at all of the exits. How can he escape us then?"

"Exactly as he has done on several occasions," replied the grocer with a sigh. "By turning himself into a bat and flying off into the night."

"That is because we have always gone up there in the hours of darkness," said Kropotel.

"Of course we have," replied Horowitz. "How better to surprise him?"

"It has always been our biggest mistake," said the police sergeant, twisting the ends of his moustache between his fingers and thumbs. "If we go up there in the daylight hours, he won't be able to become a bat. A vampire possesses the powers of transformation only during darkness. This time we will storm the castle at dawn."

"With every secret passageway's exit guarded, and with the evil one bereft of his dark satanic vampire powers – we cannot help but triumph!" Mayor Rumboll murmured, shaking slightly in gleeful anticipation of the pleasures of the vampire hunt to come.

"Even so, we must needs act quickly," said Alphonse Kropotel, folding the map carefully and buttoning it inside his uniform pocket for safe-keeping. "We shall need to go all round the village, rouse every man and have them armed and ready to steal up that mountainside before morning comes. We shall surround the castle, wait for dawn . . ." The police sergeant paused and a cruel smile spread slowly across his face as he added, gloating, "and then . . ."

"And then what, Alphonse?" asked Eric Horowitz, who was always a little slow to comprehend.

"And then the vampire will be dead!" snapped Sergeant Kropotel.

Despite the fact that it was not yet morning, Count Alucard was wide awake. Finding sleep hard to come by, he had lit the two large candles, standing on either side of his coffin in their ancient tall iron sconces, and was passing the time in pleasant fashion, sitting up in the coffin and flicking through the pages of the very latest edition of his favourite magazine, *The Coffin-Maker's Journal*.

With a birthday in the offing, Count Alucard was giving serious thought to treating himself to a brand new casket. *The Coffin-Maker's Journal*, as always, was crammed with coloured pictures showing the very latest in funereal furniture. He scanned the pages eagerly, but pulled a face when he arrived at the item granted a double-spread across the centre pages.

"A coffin made of fibre-glass! How *very* common!" he murmured to himself distastefully.

"No thank you very much. Fibre-glass may be all very well for constructing garden sheds or one-man dinghies, but when it comes to choosing a resting-place for all eternity, give me something that has been carved by a craftsman and out of lasting, solid hardwood – maple, say, or mahogany, or trusty English oak. Something that has a pleasant scent to it. Fibre-glass indeed! I sometimes wonder what this world is coming to."

With that, the count leaned over his coffin and dropped the magazine on to the stone slab floor of his dungeon. He glanced up at the small barred window high up on the wall. Outside, the black of night was dissolving into that dark grey light that comes before the dawn.

"Another half hour at least until the first glimmer of daylight," the count told himself as he snuggled down, pulling his soft white shroud up around his ears and feeling the comfort of the coffin which enclosed him by rubbing at its foot with his toes. They were those last precious minutes of darkness that Count Alucard always relished the most. For although he had not inherited his wicked ancestors' constant craving for human blood, he did possess the vampire's love of all things nocturnal.

Sometimes, when the fancy took him, Count Alucard changed himself into his fruit-bat form and spent entire nights on widespread wing, cruising the vast reaches of Tolokovin Forest with the wolf-pack loping along beneath him. He called the wolves his "children of the night". There was nothing that the count loved more than flitting through the branches of the tall fir-trees, with the wolf-pack pounding across the forest floor below.

The wolves, in their turn, relished those precious times when the count was in residence at Alucard Castle and not abroad on his travels. On nights such as this one, when he had chosen not to join them, they howled and whined and whimpered close by the castle walls in an attempt to cajole him from his coffin.

"That's very strange!" he murmured with a sudden frown.

The odd fact had occurred to him that he had not heard one single wolf howl, whine or whimper outside the castle walls for several hours. It was most unusual. Something must have happened, the count decided, to disturb the pack and to send it scampering into some other part of the forest. He decided he would investigate and find out what that "something" was.

Leaping lightly from his coffin, Count Alucard shivered as his bare feet touched the cold stone floor. He dressed himself speedily, but saw to it that his appearance was as impeccable as always: silk monogrammed boxer shorts; black silk socks; clean, crisply-ironed frilly-fronted white shirt; neatly-knotted white bow-tie; formal black well-pressed suit. And to complete his image, he slipped the precious gold medallion, which his father and grandfather had worn before him, around his neck on its fine gold chain.

He blew out both candles and, before their wicks stopped smouldering, Count Alucard had slipped out of the dungeon and was headed on his spindly legs up the worn stone steps that led towards the castle roof.

"Is everybody ready?" hissed Alphonse Kropotel, gripping his truncheon tightly and peering through the forest in the eerie half-light and the rising mist of morning. "Pass it on!"

"Sergeant Kropotel says: 'Is everybody ready?' " a voice whispered some twenty-five metres to the police sergeant's left, then added, "And he says 'Pass it on!' "

The first man to relay the message placed the makeshift weapon which he had brought along on the forest floor, then stamped his feet and slapped his arms across his chest in an attempt to keep warm. His name was Karl Gustaffe, he was Tolokovin's only baker and, if it had been up to him, he would have been enjoying the heat of his bakehouse at that moment, instead of shivering in the forest waiting for the vampire hunt to begin.

"Stop making so much noise, Gustaffe!" growled Sergeant Kropotel through the trees.

"I can't help it, Sergeant," murmured the little baker. "My teeth are chattering. I'm cold."

"Stop complaining," snarled the policeman, wandering across to where the miserable Karl Gustaffe stood. "You'd warm up soon enough if you were to feel the weight of my truncheon across your shoulders! And do stop shivering. Be a man! Pick up your weapon – I'm about to give the order to move up on the castle."

"Very good, Sergeant Kropotel," said the baker with a sigh. The sooner the vampire hunt got started, he told himself, the sooner he would be back in the warmth and comfort of his bakehouse and starting in on his daily quota of shrubel-cakes – a well-known Transylvanian delicacy.

"What's that you've got?" asked Kropotel as the baker stooped and picked up the article he had earlier put down on the ground.

"It's my rolling-pin."

"A *rolling-pin*!" gasped the policeman. "A rolling-pin against a vampire?"

"I was in my bakehouse when the summons came, Sergeant," explained the baker. "I'm an early starter. I was told to bring along a makeshift weapon. I grabbed the first thing that came to hand. It was either the rolling-pin or the egg-whisk – there wasn't anything else."

"Merciful Heaven! Whatever next?" grumbled Alphonse Kropotel. "Never mind – it will have to do. Now, call out 'Forward' to the next man along the line. And tell him to 'Pass it on'. The daylight's come at last. Time to make a start. Time to get things done."

"F-F-F-Forward!" stammered Karl Gustaffe, glancing through the fringe of trees towards where the tall, grey, imposing castle walls were looming large in the early morning light. "P-P-P-Pass it on!" the baker added nervously.

The call to advance was echoed all around the wide circle of villagers – men for the most part, but there were several tight-lipped but determined women too – who had remained concealed in the shelter of the forest which surrounded Castle Alucard. Some of the villagers were clutching sharp-pointed pitchforks, others grasped gleaming scythes, while several gripped garden hoes, the blades of which had been keenly honed. Sergeant Kropotel had taken his clumsy big revolver out of its leather holster and was waving it above his head as he strode out bravely in front brandishing his truncheon in the other hand.

Karl Gustaffe, the village baker, was not *too* concerned by the fact that he carried nothing more dangerous than a wooden rolling-pin. He had already decided that, were he to be so unlucky as to come face-to-face with the vampire, he would toss the rolling-pin aside, turn on his heel and put his faith in his legs . . .

"*Charge*!" yelled Police Sergeant Alphonse Kropotel as he moved from the safety of the trees and out on to the expanse of grass that lay between the edge of the forest and the walls of Castle Alucard.

"Death to the vampire!" screamed Henri Rumboll as he too broke from the cover of the trees, waving the hefty mayoral mace which was his choice of weapon.

"Death to all vampires!" shouted Eric Horowitz, who followed close behind the mayor, wielding the sharp, long-bladed knife he used for slicing dried goose-flesh in his grocer's shop.

Alphonse Kropotel, out in front, was spurred on at hearing his comrades' cries and further cheered by the ragged shouts that were going up on his either side. The villagers of Tolokovin, taking courage in their weight of numbers, appeared from out of the trees and broke into a stumbling run as they headed towards the castle walls, their makeshift weapons glinting in the first rays of the sun.

"Mercy me!" murmured Count Alucard, blinking in surprise as he peered nervously over the parapeted castle roof and down at where the villagers were lumbering, from all directions, across the stretch of grass towards the castle walls.

The Castle Alucard had not been built to withstand a siege. There were windows on its every side and at ground level through which attackers might easily force an entrance. Centuries before, when the count's forebears had constructed the castle, their vampire identities alone had always been sufficient to deter intruders. In olden times, a vampire's castle had been his home and no human would have dared to trespass inside its walls. But the Tolokovin peasants these days did not show the same regard for the present count as their grandfathers and great-grandfathers had shown for his own past relatives.

Count Alucard realised that, within a matter of minutes, the villagers would be swarming through every room of his ancient family home. Even so, the count was not *too* concerned. He had known several such sieges during his own lifetime. He had never had much trouble in effecting an escape before.

Leaving the castle roof, the count scampered back the way that he had come, down the worn stone winding steps as far as the ground floor. Hurrying into the library, he pressed the concealed button by the fireplace and an entire panel of old leather-bound volumes slid into the stone wall, revealing the dark secret passageway that lay beyond. But he had scarcely gone more than twenty paces along the gloomy tunnel when, to his dismay, he spotted daylight at the other end.

Could it be possible, Count Alucard wondered, that someone had discovered the exit to the secret tunnel? And as he turned this awful possibility over in his mind, he caught a glimpse of the silhouettes of two men who were waiting, at the end of the passage, to overpower him. Turning hastily on his heels – for already he could hear the urgent shouts of the villagers outside the castle walls – he darted back along the passage and out again into the library. Luckily, he knew of several other secret escape routes. His father had shown them to him as a child.

"Commit all of these to memory, my boy," the late Count Alucard had counselled his son, taking him on a tour around Castle Alucard's many concealed entrances and exits. "Guard their secret well – one day they may serve to save your life."

As the count pondered over which passageway he might attempt next, it crossed his mind that, if the villagers knew of one such exit, they might be aware of the locations of each and every other hidden tunnel . . .

"Death and destruction to the vampire!" cried a voice which, judging by its accompanying echo, came from *inside* the castle.

"Death and destruction to *all* vampires!" shouted a second voice, even closer at hand.

And then there came a swelling roar of voices as the peasants scrambled in through windows all around the castle.

Panicking now, and fearful of risking another secret passage, Count Alucard seized at the only option that was open to him and set off, in haste, out of the library. He sprinted on his long thin legs back up the circular stone stairway which led only to the roof – from which there was no escape . . .

Hearing the murmur of many voices close behind him on the stone steps, buzzing like a storm of angry wasps, the count gained himself some short respite by bolting the stout iron-studded door before he walked out on to the castle roof. Crossing to the parapet, the count let out a long despairing sigh as he gazed out across the tree-tops. Out there, he told himself, lay freedom – but there was no way down the castle walls. Neither was there an exit from the castle roof, except by way of the door through which he had just come and on the other side of which a whole horde of villagers was now clamouring for his life.

"Fetch up a floorboard or a bench!" he heard one voice call out, louder than the rest, which he recognised as that of his old enemy, Police Sergeant Alphonse Kropotel. "We'll soon break down this door!"

"And bring up a mallet and a sharp-pointed wooden stake!" cried out another voice which, Count Alucard knew, belonged to Henri Rumboll, the Mayor of Tolokovin.

"That's it! That's it!" cried out a third excited voice which the count had no difficulty in identifying as that of Eric Horowitz, the village shopkeeper. "We'll drive a sharp-pointed wooden stake through the evil monster's heart – that's the way to deal with vampires!"

And then all of the single voices on the other side of the iron-studded door were lost in the general frenzied hubbub.

Count Alucard sighed again and sadly shook his head. In his entire life, he had never ever knowingly harmed a single living thing – and yet, because he had been born an Alucard, it seemed that every man's hand was turned against him. Sitting down on the parapet, the count's shoulders drooped dispiritedly as he prepared to meet his end. Nothing could save him now, he told himself – except, perhaps, a miracle.

2

"Ouch!" cried Mr Hollins, crossly, as he jarred his shin in the dark.

"Are you all right, Albert?" Emily Hollins' anxious words drifted down towards her husband from the bedroom overhead.

"Absolutely!" Albert Hollins called back. "Except that I've just given myself another almighty crack on the corner of this thumping great coffin!"

"Oh dear!" exclaimed Mrs Hollins sympathetically.

"Oh dear indeed!" murmured Mr Hollins to himself, as his fumbling fingers located at last what they had been seeking – the empty cocoa cups which had been resting, since the previous night, on coasters on the coffin lid.

Although Count Alucard's polished, dark-wood, second-best coffin had held pride of place in the Hollins family's living-room for many months now, Mr Hollins was still prone to bump into it, in the dark of the early morning, when he wandered around downstairs prior to making a first cup of tea. And although Albert Hollins had cracked his shin at the very same moment that Count Alucard had sat down despondently on his castle roof, there were so many miles between them that, while the sun was up in Transylvania, it was still dark in the Hollins' home in the north of England.

Perhaps we should pause long enough from our story at this point, to explain why the Transylvanian vegetarian vampire's second-best coffin stood in the living-room at 42, Nicholas Nickleby Close, Staplewood.

Henry Hollins, Mr and Mrs Hollins's young son, is Count Alucard's best friend. They first met some time ago now, when the Hollinses had lost their way while on a camping holiday in Europe and had ended up, one spooky, moonlit night, outside the count's castle. Henry Hollins and Count Alucard had struck up an instant friendship. Since that lucky chance encounter, they have shared several exciting adventures: at a circus, by the seaside, at a magicians' conference, in a vampire theme park – and even in the gardens at Buckingham Palace. In fact, the pair are such exceptional friends that Count Alucard has seen fit to leave his second-best coffin at Henry's home, in order that he will have somewhere comfortable to lay his head should he ever chance to spend the night in Staplewood.

You might think that Emily Hollins, Henry's mother, would object to having a Transylvanian vampire's coffin set down in her living-room, but only if you did not know that lady at all well. Far from being put out by the coffin, Mrs Hollins is delighted by its presence. Not only does it serve as an unusual coffee-table – and a talking-point when neighbours come to call – the dark polished wood is a perfect match for the upright piano which stands against the living-room wall.

It does, however, present some small inconvenience to Albert Hollins, who is inclined to forget that the coffin is there if he should chance to be in the living-room and in the dark.

"Oooooh!" roared Mr Hollins, letting out a cry of pain for the second time that morning.

"What is it this time, Albert?" called down Emily Hollins from the bedroom.

"I've stubbed my big toe this time on the corner of this confounded coffin!" yelled Mr Hollins, hopping on one foot as he attempted to massage his aching toe through his slipper while, at the same time, trying not to lose his hold on the three used cocoa cups and saucers balanced in the other hand.

"Hush, Albert!" hissed Emily through the ceiling. "You'll wake up Henry."

But Henry Hollins was not asleep. He was not even in his bed. Having been disturbed from his slumbers by his father's first anguished cries of pain, Henry Hollins had slipped out from underneath his duvet, tiptoed across to the window and drawn back the curtain as the sun (already shining brightly in far-off Transylvania) cast its first golden rays across sleepy Staplewood. Henry Hollins gazed out across his back garden where, it seemed, a perky garden gnome peered back at him from around every bush and shrub and tub of plants.

Albert Hollins worked at Staplewood Garden Gnomes Ltd, a factory which was famous throughout the world, and where he held the important post of Assistant Head of the Packing

and Despatch Department. Because of his position, Mr Hollins was allowed to buy the company's products at wholesale prices. Albert Hollins took full advantage of this opportunity and, as a consequence, both the front and back gardens at 42, Nicholas Nickleby Close were dotted with small, grinning, red-cheeked, white-bearded plastic garden gnomes. Indeed, had Albert had his way, the garden gnomes would have infiltrated the house. He had once gone so far as to try to put a garden gnome at either end of the living-room mantelpiece. But Emily Hollins had put her foot down very firmly on that account.

"No, Albert," Emily had stated, shaking her head slowly. "You can put as many gnomes as your heart desires outside in the garden. I'm very partial to a gnome myself – in its proper place. Why, there is nothing nicer, in springtime, than to see a couple of garden gnomes peeping through the daffodils. But there's a proper place for everything, Albert, and a garden gnome belongs in the garden." At which point Emily Hollins had paused, wrinkled her nose as she sought to express her thoughts aloud, and then added, "If God had intended garden gnomes to go inside the home, he would have given them comfy chairs to sit on – not red-and-yellow plastic spotted mushrooms."

On which wise words, the subject was considered closed.

But it was not the garden gnomes that filled Henry Hollins's thoughts on that particular morning. Looking past his back garden across the house-tops, Henry was staring out at where the sun was slowly rising over the towering Civic Centre, the vast many-storied concrete car-park, and the white-slab windowless building that was Staplewood's Town Hall.

Somewhere in that direction, Henry told himself, but many, many miles beyond, lay distant Transylvania. Henry Hollins was wondering what his friend, Count Alucard, was doing that morning. Perhaps it was just as well Henry could not know that, at the exact same moment, Count Alucard's very life was threatened. For, even if he had been aware of his friend's unfortunate predicament, there was nothing that Henry could have done to save the situation . . .

The clamour on the other side of the stout iron-studded door at the top of the castle's winding, worn, stone staircase, had turned from shouts of frustrated anger to cries of eager approval, accompanying the regular sounds of an axe-head crashing into splintering wood.

"Again, Emil!" cried a voice which the count recognised as Alphonse Kropotel's. "Another couple of well-aimed blows and we'll have the evil villain in our clutches!"

Count Alucard guessed that the "Emil" the police sergeant was urging on to greater efforts was none other than Emil Gruff, the local woodcutter who was famed throughout the district for his destructive prowess with an axe.

The surly, scruffy woodcutter and Count Alucard were old adversaries. For one thing, the count loved to roam the forest, and could never see eye-to-eye with a man whose main ambition was to chop down every tree for miles around. More important, though, when Gruff was not at work with his axe, he was busy setting wolf-traps in every glade and thicket. The woodcutter was sure – although he could not prove it – that it was none other than the count himself who scoured the forest at first light, springing the traps that he had gone to so much trouble to lay down.

But although Count Alucard was usually successful in foiling Emil Gruff's attempts at catching the wolves, there could be no denying the woodcutter's skills with his sharp-bladed shiny axe. Even as Count Alucard watched, there came another thunderous blow from the other side of the door, louder than those that had gone before, and this time the keen blade penetrated the wood.

Count Alucard gulped and shivered. Any second now, he told himself, the door must burst on its rusty hinges underneath the woodcutter's fierce attack, and then there would be nothing between himself and the angry blood-thirsting mob.

Several moments before, the count had hoped for a miracle. What happened next may not have been a miracle in the true sense of the word – but it proved to be all that Count Alucard could ever have hoped to expect. By this time, the morning sun had crept over the mountain rim and was making steady upward progress into a clear blue sky. All at once, a dark low-lying storm cloud appeared, as if out of nowhere, and drifted across the face of the sun. Daylight turned instantly into the dark of night.

Count Alucard's low spirits soared. The change from dawn to darkness – even though it would provide no more than a temporary respite – was sufficient, the count told himself, to grant him use of his vampire powers. Provided he acted upon it speedily! Stretching his lanky legs, Count Alucard sprang up sure-footedly on to the castle's parapet.

At that same instant, the door flew open. With Sergeant Kropotel leading the way, brandishing his truncheon, and followed close behind by the axe-wielding Emil Gruff, the angry mob surged out on to the roof. They pulled up short at the sight of Count Alucard perched fearlessly on the parapet.

"Seize him!" cried Alphonse Kropotel, guessing what was about to happen.

But before the mob could make a move, and although not one single drop of rain had fallen, the sky was suddenly split by a lightning bolt which zig-zagged from the storm cloud to the castle's roof, accompanied by a deafening crash of thunder.

"Aaaaah. . . .!" A fearful murmur went up from the Tolokovinites who, instead of rushing forward at Sergeant Kropotel's command, pressed back upon themselves, those at the front treading on the toes of those who came behind.

Balanced on the parapet, Count Alucard took a firm hold with both of his hands on his crimson-lined black cloak and spread it wide on either side of his body. Then, as the peasants gazed open-mouthed in wonder, the count launched himself from off the castle's towering wall and into the dark of that mysterious false night.

For a moment or two – although it seemed much longer to those who watched – Count Alucard hovered on his outstretched cape, held suspended by an upward wind. And then a weird and wonderful transformation happened. The count's black-cloaked body seemed to shrivel up as he turned himself into a small, furry-bodied, snub-nosed, sharp-eared creature with black twinkling eyes; hovering, for all to see, on widespread, membraneous parchment-like wings.

Count Alucard, now in his vegeterian vampire fruit-bat form, fluttered in front of the gawping Tolokovinite peasants for several seconds, happy at being airborne and pausing only long enough to get the feel of his wings before darting off below the level of the castle roof and out of sight.

"Aaah-AAAH. . . .!" The vampire hunters sighed again, louder this time than before, but still without moving, as though rooted where they stood.

"You fools!" stormed Alphonse Kropotel, ign-

oring the fact that he himself had stood as statue-like as all of the others during Count Alucard's transformation. "Get down those steps and get after him! It will be light again in a moment – the monster must change back then into human shape!"

But to Sergeant Kropotel's further dismay, several precious seconds more were lost as Henri Rumboll and Eric Horowitz – who had stayed, for safety's sake, at the back of the throng during the storming of the castle roof – now jammed the narrow doorway with their portly bodies as they turned together and both attempted to squeeze through at once. Tolokovin's mayor and shop-keeper both huffed and puffed and breathed in deeply in unison as they tried to draw in their ample stomachs, but all to no effect, while Alphonse Kropotel fumed and fretted at the back of the throng of pressing peasants.

At last their efforts were rewarded and both Henri Rumboll and Eric Horowitz shot out, simultaneously, on the other side of the doorway, like two corks popping out of the same bottle. Learning their lesson from the two who had gone before, the other Tolokovinites sped through the doorway in single file, with Sergeant Kropotel bringing up the rear.

Needing no further urging, the vampire hunters raced down the circular stairway. The only sounds that could be heard were the urgent scuffle of many feet on the worn stone stairs and the short sharp complaining pants from the less fit, stouter members of the bloodthirsty band.

As the dark cloud drifted on its way as quickly as it had come, leaving the sun to shine in an otherwise cloudless sky, Count Alucard became aware of the growing weight of his human body as the transformation was reversed.

Thankfully, anticipating the change, he had already reduced his altitude and was gliding on outstretched wing no more than a couple of metres above the ground when, unable to help himself, he was turned back from vegetarian vampire bat to Transylvanian count. Easing down the lower half of his body, with the feel of his outstretched cape in both of his hands, he allowed himself a little sigh of relief as his shiny black patent-leather shoes touched ground together. A couple of strides on his lanky legs before coming to a halt and he had executed a perfect landing.

Glancing over his shoulder, the count could see the towering walls of Alucard Castle some hundred metres and more away, while the dark safety of the wide-ranging forest lay only a few short metres ahead.

"*Ah-whoo-OOOOH. . . .!*"

Count Alucard smiled to himself at the sound of the wolf-call which had come from just inside the forest. He recognised the call as having been made by Boris, wily old pack-leader and the count's close friend. At the same moment, he heard the distant yells of the vampire hunters as they burst out through the castle gates, waving their makeshift weapons over their heads and storming across the grass in his direction.

In seconds, Count Alucard had sought the shelter of the forest.

"Spread out, men!" bellowed Sergeant Kropotel, in the vain hope of turning his ill-assorted rabble into a well-ordered army as they approached the first line of trees. "Form yourselves into a human chain and advance into the forest in one long line!" Nobody paid him the slightest attention. "There's a purseful of grubecks for the man who runs the monster down to earth!" the sergeant added as a last resort.

But even the promise of financial gain had no effect on the usually greedy villagers. Their faces flushed and their tempers raised at having run first up, then down the castle's several hundred winding stone steps, they were in no mood to listen to reason. They charged into the forest in undisciplined fashion, shouting insults and hurling threats. Emil Gruff, the bearded woodcutter, was at the forefront, screaming wild oaths and swinging his long-handled axe in circles over his head.

Three men, lacking the enthusiasm of their fellows, stumbled along unhappily at the rear.

Mayor Henri Rumboll was fast losing his appetite for the vampire hunt. He had no wish to pursue Count Alucard into the forest. It had been all very well out in the open, where there had been strength and comfort to be gained from numbers. But the mayor had sense enough to realise that, once inside the dark of the towering trees, he might very easily lose contact with the others. He shivered at the very idea. Henri Rumboll had no desire to come face-to-face with a pointy-toothed vampire while he was on his own.

Karl Gustaffe, the little baker, had not had any spirit for the vampire hunt from the very beginning. Press-ganged into taking part, he had more important matters to attend to. There were the several big stone pots, full of dough, that he had left back in the warmth of the bakehouse. It should be nicely risen by now. If it was not cut and rolled and shaped into two hundred shrubel-cakes, the dough might very well spoil.

Eric Horowitz, the village shopkeeper and third member of the trio, was much too hot and far too tired to struggle any further. Besides, he asked himself, where was the sense in running at full tilt into the darkness of the trees and across the forest's uneven floor while carrying the keen-bladed goose-knife? Supposing he were to trip over a fallen branch or put his foot into a rabbit-hole, then fall upon the sharp point of the knife . . .? The shop-keeper shivered at the awful thought.

Stooping, Eric Horowitz put his hands upon his knees and struggled to regain his breath. He sneaked a glance at his two companions who, it seemed, were similarly short of wind. Ahead of them, from out of the forest, came the urgent shouts of the vampire hunters who were already struggling to keep in contact with one another.

"How would it be," ventured the shopkeeper, "if, instead of joining the others, we were to make our own way back to the village and wait for them to return?"

"That sounds like an excellent idea to me!" said Karl Gustaffe, nodding eagerly. "There are more than enough of them in the forest already. And you know the old Transylvanian saying: 'One baker can easily make five hundred shrubel-cakes, but two bakers cannot make one shrubel-cake without stepping on each other's toes'."

Horowitz and Gustaffe looked anxiously at Henri Rumboll, waiting for his decision. Rumboll, after all, *was* the Mayor of Tolokovin and his would be the final word.

"Agreed," said Rumboll, taking a firm grip on his mace and turning his back on the forest. "We'll go back to the village hall. Once the vampire is captured, they're sure to take him there."

Skirting the edge of the forest, Henri Rumboll,

Karl Gustaffe and Eric Horowitz set off, walking towards the mountain road which wandered down towards the sleepy village of Tokovin.

"*Ah-whoo-OOO-ooooh . . .!*"

The three men quickened their pace at the sound of the wolf-howl from deep in the forest and, at the same time, the shouts of the vampire hunters increased in urgency.

"If you ask me," said Karl Gustaffe, with a sniff, "I don't think they'll catch the vampire."

But whether either Henri Rumboll, Tolokovin's mayor, or Eric Horowitz, the shopkeeper, agreed with the village baker on this matter was not to be revealed – for neither of them ventured an opinion.

The three men plodded on, thankfully downhill, in silence.

3

"Good morning, Algernon!"

The red-cheeked, white-bearded little garden gnome, standing with a spade poised in the herbaceous border, made no reply to the greeting – partly because "Algernon" was not its name but more importantly, perhaps, because it was made of plastic.

Arthur Shepherd, the postman, who had bade the garden gnome "Good morning!" was not at all put out at being met with silence. For one thing, he *knew* that the gnome wasn't real and secondly, he was well aware that its name wasn't Algernon. Algernon was the name that Arthur Shepherd had given to it, as a joke. Mr Shepherd had made up names for all of the gnomes in the Hollins's front garden and, as he strode up the crazy-paving path (recently laid down by Albert Hollins) that led to the front door, he called out a "Good morning" or a "Nice day" or a "Lovely weather for the time of year!" to each and every one of them.

Postman Shepherd looked forward eagerly to delivering the mail each day at 42, Nicholas Nickleby Close. Similarly he was disappointed on those days when there wasn't a letter to be popped through the Hollins' letter-box. On that particular morning there were *three* letters for the Hollins household. One of them, which was addressed to Henry Hollins in black ink and in neat if slightly spidery handwriting, had a curious Transylvanian stamp on the top right-hand corner.

The second envelope, larger than the first, was addressed to "Mr Albert Hollins", carried a London postmark and had a printed logo across the top which announced the contents: *The Garden Gnome Collector's Monthly.* The third envelope, also posted in London, was for "Mrs Emily Hollins", and had the title: *The Wheatie-Snax Breakfast Cereal Co. (Inc.)* printed across the top in glistening golden letters.

Arthur Shepherd frowned as he popped the mail through the Hollins' letter-flap, and wondered why a world-famous breakfast cereal company would write a letter to a Staplewood housewife. But it was a postman's lot in life, he told himself as he retraced his steps along the garden path, to deliver all manner of intriguing letters through any number of letter-flaps – and never to learn the nature of the contents. And then he smiled, for Postman Shepherd *did* know how eagerly Mr Hollins looked forward every month to receiving his magazine and, also, how delighted Henry Hollins was by his occasional letters from Transylvania. Being a postman, Arthur Shepherd reminded himself, was a pleasant occupation to have, for he was responsible for bringing pleasure to so many people . . .

"Toodle-pip, lads!" the postman called over his

shoulder at the garden gnomes as he closed the gate behind him. "Have a nice day!" he added.

"Woof Woof!" barked Gringo, the Irish wolfhound at Number 44, bounding out of his kennel and across the lawn at the sound of the postman's approaching footsteps.

"Hello, Gringo," said Arthur Shepherd warily, as he pushed open the garden gate.

"WOOF! WOOF! WOOF!" barked Gringo, leaping up excitedly and planting both of his front paws firmly on the postman's chest.

"Here we go again!" sighed Arthur Shepherd as he staggered backwards. Big, bounding, barking dogs were one of those things that a postman had to put up with on his daily rounds. "Down, Gringo!" urged Postman Shepherd. "Down, boy! Down!"

"I've won!" cried Emily Hollins in delight, as she quickly scanned the contents of the letter from the breakfast cereal company. "I've won a prize in the Wheatie-Snax competition!"

"Well done, that woman," said Albert Hollins as

he poured milk over his bowl of Wheatie-Snax. "Does that mean that we won't have to eat any more of these ghastly things?" he added hopefully.

"Not once we've finished off what we've got, Albert," said Emily.

In order to enter the cereal company's competition, it had been necessary to enclose with every entry, a coupon cut out from the back of a Wheatie-Snax packet. Emily Hollins, who made quite a hobby out of going in for competitions, had sent off several entries in an attempt to win one of the many exciting Wheatie-Snax prizes. This had meant that both Albert and Henry had been dutifully eating the "honey-coated, sultana-sprinkled" breakfast cereal every morning, week after week. Sometimes, in order to speed up their consumption, Emily had been serving Wheatie-Snax as a suppertime treat – and even, on the odd occasion, as a lunch-time pudding.

Albert Hollins, who was not all that fond of honey and disliked sultanas intensely, was overjoyed at hearing that his Wheatie-Snax devouring duties were almost at an end.

"Jolly good," said Albert.

"I'm pleased you're pleased, Albert," said Emily Hollins, with a secretive little smile.

What Albert Hollins was not to know – and what Emily intended on keeping from him at that moment – was that there was a stockpile of six family-size packets of Wheatie-Snax waiting to be eaten, all with their competiton coupons already removed, tucked away on the top shelf of the larder. Another surprise that Mrs Hollins was keeping from her husband was that the prize she had won from the Wheatie-Snax Company was a jumbo-size packet of Wheatie-Snax.

Mr Hollins, however, was not all that interested in hearing about Emily's prize that morning. He had come across an item in the new issue of *The Garden Gnome Collector's Monthly* that was *much* more exciting. It was something that, for the time being, he intended to keep to himself.

Henry Hollins, at that same moment, had his own surprise in store. He was upstairs in his bedroom, sitting on the end of his bed and poring over the letter that he had received that morning from far-off Transylvania. It had come, of course, from Count Alucard, the vegetarian vampire himself.

There was no mention in the letter of that morning's storming of Castle Alucard. How could there have been? The count had written it in happier times, some several days before, when he had had no inkling of Police Sergeant Kropotel's evil plan.

> *Henry, my dear good friend,*
>
> *As I sit here by candlelight and comfortably in my coffin, sipping at my bed-time glass of tomato juice, my thoughts are turning constantly to you. Outside my window, from somewhere not too far off in the forest, I can hear the howling of the wolf-pack calling out to me. Very soon, I shall put down my pen, spread my wings and go to join my children of the night.*
>
> *Before I do, I felt the need to drop this short note to your dear, kind parents and yourself,*

inviting the three of you to take a plane, come out here and holiday with me at Castle Alucard. I know how much you would enjoy yourselves. It is that time of year when the forest floor is thick with flowers, the warm afternoon air filled with the buzzing of bees and heavy with the scent of pine.

Do say yes! Do write back soon! Do come out quickly. I am so eager to share some part of this glorious Transylvanian summer with you. I know that I can promise you a simply heavenly time!

Warmest regards as always,
Count Alucard

"Brilliant!" cried Henry Hollins, jumping joyfully into the air and off his bed.

Downstairs in the kitchen, Emily and Albert Hollins glanced up at the ceiling, puzzled, as they heard Henry's feet thud loudly on the floor above their heads. A moment later, they heard him clattering down the stairs.

"Mum! Dad!" he cried, bursting into the kitchen and waving the letter from Count Alucard above his head. "Just you wait until you hear about this!"

Mrs and Mrs Hollins exchanged a little smile. They knew that Henry had had a letter from the count that morning. They had already guessed at the news the envelope had contained. They had an alternative suggestion that they had discussed, and which they now intended to propose to Henry . . .

Standing close to the pine tree's trunk, hugging its

shadow, Count Alucard stood very still and listened hard. There was no doubt about it. The murmur of voices and the sounds of movement in the undergrowth were getting closer by the second. What was worse, they seemed to be coming from all directions. He was surrounded.

Sergeant Alphonse Kropotel, kneeling down behind a clump of bracken, allowed himself a little smile of self-satisfaction. It had been difficult; it had taken time; it had been necessary for him to curse, to shout, to threaten and to bully – but he had finally succeeded in organising his rabble band into some sort of disciplined order. What was more, he felt quite sure that he finally had the evil-hearted monster in his grasp.

The police sergeant took a tight grip on the mallet that he held in one hand and an even tighter hold on the sharp-pointed wooden stake which was in the other. He had taken these two instruments of vampire destruction from the two villagers who had brought them along. When it was time for the vampire to meet its end, Kropotel had decided that it would be he who delivered the final blows, not any other man.

Raising the mallet above his head and over the bracken, the police sergeant waved it slowly in a circle, signalling that the circle of vampire hunters was to draw in even closer. This time there would be no escape for the vampire count of Castle Alucard.

Count Alucard had one trick left up his sleeve. Still standing in the shadow of the broad tree trunk, he glanced down at the four-footed animal at his side. Boris, the wily leader of the wolf-pack, panted softly, as he gazed back enquiringly at the count. The old wolf nuzzled his greying head into Count Alucard's welcoming hand and waited for instructions.

Some time before, when the count had first sought sanctuary in the wide-reaching forest, he had been joined in an instant by the entire wolf-pack who had anticipated his arrival. Rather than have any of the wolves injured unnecessarily by the blood-thirsty villagers, Count Alucard had ordered the wolves to take flight. They had obeyed this order without question, scampering off into the shadowy dark without so much as a whimper – with one exception. Boris, the old campaigner, had remained behind with the count's permission.

Count Alucard smiled fondly, and stroked at the loose fur underneath the old wolf's jowls. If ever danger threatened – as it did at that moment – the count would rather have had Boris at his side than any human being. Now, and not for the first time in his eventful life, Count Alucard was about to call upon the pack-leader's loyalty and guile.

"*Drushka, Boris!*" whispered Count Alucard. "*Drushka – drobna shnuk!*"

Obeying these instructions to the letter, Boris sped off between the trees and through the undergrowth, keeping his grey head dipped and out of sight, but making as much noise as he could. There was sufficient distance between the villagers who made up the circle for the old wolf to pass easily between them without anyone catching sight of anything – except a rustle in a patch of long grass that skirted a forest stream.

"That way! He went that way!" cried Emil Gruff, whose woodsman's keen ears had been the first to pick up on the sound of Boris crashing through the bracken, and whose sharp eyes now marked the movement in the undergrowth as the wolf raced past. "Follow me!" he urged. "We'll soon catch up with the evil-hearted monster!"

Circling his gleaming axe above his head, the woodcutter lurched off through the trees in pursuit of what he believed to be the vampire, waving at the villagers to follow him. Taking him at his word, the vampire hunters of Tolokovin broke out of their hiding places and lumbered after Emil Gruff.

"Wait! Wait, all of you!" shouted Alphonse Kropotel, suspecting trickery, as his carefully planned circle of men broke up in confusion for the second time that morning.

But the police sergeant's pleas fell on deaf ears. The villagers were already disappearing among the trees. Kropotel was left with no alternative except to set off himself in pursuit of his band of vampire hunters, threatening and cajoling them in turn to ignore the cries of Emil Gruff and to obey his own instructions.

Moments later, when both the vampire hunters and their angry leader had gone off on the wild-goose chase on which Boris was leading them, Count Alucard stepped out from behind the tall pine tree. He smiled as his eyes took in the empty forest.

"Well done, old friend!" he murmured. Then, heading in the opposite direction to the one taken by his pursuers, the count set off at an easy pace until he too was quickly out of sight. The far-reaching forest returned to a silence that was broken only occasionally by the sound of bird-song.

"Good day to you, Count Alucard!"

The words were almost drowned by the sound of creaking wheels; the count turned, not only at the greeting, but also to take note of the gaily coloured, horse-drawn caravan which was overtaking him along the forest track.

"Good-day to you too, Serafina Krokulengro!" he called back at the grey-haired, black-eyed, weather-beaten, wrinkled gypsy woman who was crouched on the driving seat.

Almost an hour had gone by since the failed ambush. Having kept up the steady pace at which he had started out, Count Alucard guessed that he had put three kilometres and more between himself and his pursuers. There was ample time, he told himself, to stop for a breather and pass the time of the day with the old gypsy woman.

"Whoa there, Petra!" Serafina Krokulengro tugged at the reins and the horse whinnied as it came to a stop.

Count Alucard had known the old woman all his life. She had known his father too, and his father's father before him. No one knew the gypsy's age but it was rumoured that she had seen more than a hundred summers come and go.

The old woman had spent her entire life on the road, travelling all over Central Europe and sometimes even further afield. But her journeyings always brought her back to Transylvania, the country where she had been born. And whenever Serafina was in the district of Tolokovin, she never failed to call at the Castle Alucard, where she could always rely upon the kindness of Count Alucard for a kettle's filling of clear water and a morsel of food or a handful of vegetables for her cooking-pot.

She was equally careful, though, to stay well clear of the village of Tolokovin. Police Sergeant Kropotel despised gypsy folk almost as much as he hated vampires. Why, only a week or so ago, when the old gypsy woman had been camped in a forest clearing, carving clothes-pegs, fashioning bunches of lucky white heather and harming no one, Alphonse Kropotel had burst upon her, overturned the cooking-pot and searched the caravan. He had, the old woman remembered, gone off with some sort of map that he had found beneath the floorboards, the existence of which she had not even been aware.

"Where are you going, Count Alucard?" asked the old woman, dismissing the encounter with the police sergeant from her mind.

"I only wish I knew, Serafina," replied the count with a long, slow sigh.

One thing was certain, he told himself, he could not go back to Castle Alucard. Sergeant Kropotel would be sure to have guards posted outside the ancient walls for several weeks to come, in the hope

that Count Alucard might return to his home. On the other hand, if he was not able to return to Castle Alucard, where *could* he go? The count had left the castle in such a hurry that he had quite forgotten to bring any money. His every single grubeck was contained inside the purse which he had tucked away the night before, for safety, inside the foot of his coffin. And that was another matter that caused him grave concern. How could he go anywhere when his coffin was contained in Castle Alucard's deepest dungeon? Why, the very idea was unthinkable!

If he can possibly avoid it, Count Alucard never spends a single night away from his castle without his coffin. Some people have security blankets; the count has his shiny black, silver-handled coffin. Ever since he first came into the world – on a rain-swept Transylvanian night, when the black sky was split with lightning flashes and the castle shook with the rumble of thunder – Count Alucard has slept inside a coffin. Without the comfort of four solid wooden coffin walls around him and, sometimes, with the lid shut tight on top, he finds sleep impossible. Whenever circumstances dictate that the count must spend a night in an ordinary bed, he tosses, turns, squirms and fidgets until dawn peeps over the horizon.

Of course, the count reminded himself, there was his second-best coffin which he had left, in case of such an emergency, in the living-room at 42, Nicholas Nickleby Close, in the little English town of Staplewood. If he could only make his way there, he knew that he could count on his good friend, Henry Hollins, for food and shelter. But to travel as far as England, he would need to have money in his pocket. He could not return to the castle for his purse; neither could he continue on his way without so much as a half-grubeck to his name . . .

Count Alucard let out another long, vexed sigh as his problems turned full circle in his head.

"Whatever it is that troubles thee, Count Alucard, shall not be solved by standing in this forest and fretting over it," said the old gypsy woman, her voice breaking in on the count's thoughts.

"You are right, Serafina Krokulengro!" replied the count, suddenly arriving at a decision. "May I beg a ride with you?"

The gypsy nodded and then jerked her head, indicating that the count clamber up beside her on the wooden seat. "Where are you bound for?" she asked, once he was perched at her side.

"As far beyond this forest as I am able to travel before nightfall," announced the count and then, spreading his hands out wide, palms upward, he shrugged his slim shoulders hopelessly as he added, "And then I am in the hands of fortune – and who knows where they may carry me?"

"As to the first part of that statement, I am able to assist thee, Count Alucard, for I am myself intending to put this forest far behind me before dark," said the old gypsy woman with a chuckle. "But with regard to where Dame Fortune may take you, I know not – for I know not whither I am bound myself!"

With which, still cackling quietly to herself, Serafina Krokulengro shook the reins, the old horse started up and the caravan lumbered off between the trees along the rutted cart-track.

"*Ah-whoo-OOOH-oooooh*!" A wolf howled somewhere off in the distance.

4

"Not go to Transylvania?" wailed Henry Hollins, gazing glumly at Count Alucard's letter which he was still clutching, tightly, in one hand. "Why not?" he added, his shoulders drooping even further. "We've been invited."

"I'm sure that it was very kind of Count Alucard to ask us to visit him at his castle, Henry," said Mrs Hollins, trying hard not to shiver at the thought of mice droppings and spiders' webs. "And you must sit down and write back to him straight away and thank him very kindly for his generous offer. But the thing is, your dad and I have been putting our heads together and we've come to the very definite conclusion that it would be nice if, for once, we were to spend a holiday at home."

"Holiday at home, Mum?" said Henry Hollins, aghast.

"Right here in Staplewood," said Albert Hollins, smiling broadly and rubbing his hands together in anticipation of the pleasures that such a holiday would bring.

"But we *always* go away on holiday," said Henry, puzzled. "We never *ever* stay at home."

Henry Hollins had spoken the truth. What was

more, the Hollins' family holidays had always provided them with all kinds of unexpected adventures. They had been to Transylvania twice before and, on both of these occasions, had met up with all kinds of vampirical excitements. On another annual holiday, a trip to the little English seaside town of Scarcombe had provided them with more thrills than some people might expect from a world cruise. Their most exciting holiday of all, perhaps – certainly from Mr Hollins's point of view – had been the weekend they had spent in London. On this never-to-be-forgotten visit, Albert Hollins had been turned (but only temporarily, thank goodness!) into a horrible hairy werewolf.

It was, perhaps, as a result of these and several other spooky holiday adventures that Mr and Mrs Hollins had decided to spend this year's summer holiday in the peace and comfort of their own home.

"A nice quiet couple of weeks doing absolutely nothing except pottering about in the garden will suit me down to the ground," observed Albert with a contented sigh. "There are a couple of new garden gnomes I'd like to get cemented into place down by the pond."

"And a fortnight at home will just fill the bill too as far as I'm concerned," said Emily Hollins, glancing across in the direction of the living-room. "I've been intending to give that coffin a thorough going-over and a good polish for a couple of months now – and the inside could do with a couple of coats of anti-woodworm treatment. You never know when it might be needed."

"It won't be needed this year, Mum," said Henry Hollins. "Count Alucard isn't coming here – he's invited *us* to go to Transylvania to see *him*."

But Albert and Emily Hollins had made up their minds. It was to be a holiday at home, without any undue excitements, for the Hollins family that summer. Henry Hollins, realising that further attempts at trying to change his parents' plans would get him nowhere, tucked the letter from his Transylvanian friend into his back pocket, poured milk over his bowl of Wheatie-Snax, and munched at his breakfast in silence.

"Do you mean to stand there, Alphonse Kropotel, and tell me that you've allowed that evil-hearted monster to escape *again*?" snapped Henri Rumboll.

Police Sergeant Kropotel shrugged bad-temperedly and tugged fiercely at his moustache between thumb and forefinger. Eric Horowitz, sitting between his two companions, glanced anxiously at both of their faces in turn.

The three men had met up again on the same morning of the fruitless vampire hunt in the market-square of Tolokovin, underneath the statue of Saint Unfortunato, the village's patron saint. (Unfortunato had been an unlucky chap, who in days gone by had had both his arms and legs chopped off by unkindly folk and whose picture now hung on the wall in every humble village home.) In order to review the situation in private, where their conversation would not be overheard, Kropotel, Rumboll and Horowitz had retired to the storeroom behind Horowitz's general shop. The shopkeeper had put the CLOSED card in the shop door's glass panel and turned the key in the lock.

Henri Rumboll and Alphonse Kropotel were sitting on sacks of chicken-feed while Horowitz was perched, uncomfortably, on a hard, sharp-cornered wooden crate containing jars of lamp-oil. A dozen or so long, dark, smoked, garlic-flavoured sausages hung from the oak-beamed ceiling. The strong smell from the garlic sausages mingled with the stench of sweating goat's cheese.

"It wasn't my fault that the monster slipped through our net," growled the police sergeant at last. "He managed to make a fool of all of us – you two were as much to blame as I was."

"Neither Horowitz nor myself happens to be the Police Sergeant of Tolokovin," replied Mayor Rumboll. "You are the man responsible for law and order in this village. And yet every time you lead a vampire-hunting party up that mountain, it seems you come back from the castle empty-handed."

"Nobody ever said that catching vampires was easy," growled Kropotel, wriggling his broad backside on the sack beneath him. Then, when the chicken-feed inside the sack had arranged itself into a shape that better suited the police sergeant's ample rear, he continued with a shrug, "What does it matter anyway? In a month or so, the villagers will have totally forgotten about this morning's fiasco."

"That's true," said Eric Horowitz, nodding eagerly.

"In a month or so, Sergeant," said Mayor

Rumboll, frowning, "the vampire will return from his travels, as he always does, to take up residence again in Alucard Castle – and the whole tiresome business will begin again."

"That's also true," said the shopkeeper, who always seemed to agree with whatever the last person to speak had said. Then, glancing up through the storeroom's small skylight at the dark outline of the castle high on the mountainside, silhouetted by the mid-morning sun, which seemed to overshadow all of their lives, he said solemnly, "It's high time someone did something to put an end to the problem once and for always."

"Oh? And what do you suggest then, Eric Horowitz?" demanded Sergeant Kropotel.

"I don't know," replied the shopkeeper doubtfully. He paused. His forehead wrinkled in thought for several seconds before he added, "But *somebody* should do *something*."

"Exactly!" cried Mayor Rumboll. "And I'll tell you what *we're* going to do," he continued, his eyes narrowing as he stared hard at Alphonse Kropotel. "Instead of just sitting here, as we've always done in the past, waiting for the vampire to return to the castle whenever takes its fancy – *we're* going to take the initiative. We're going to send someone out into the world to track the monster down and, once they've found it, drive a wooden stake through its heart right there on the spot."

Alphonse Kropotel, aware of the mayor's unblinking gaze, shuffled his bottom for a second time and the chicken-feed rustled uneasily underneath him. "I hope you're not suggesting that I should be the one to go?"

"Why not?" said Henri Rumboll grumpily.

"Why not?" echoed Eric Horowitz.

"Impossible. I've more than enough on my plate, thank you very much, here in the village. Who would attend to the wrong-doers if I was not around?"

"What wrong-doers?" snapped the mayor. "When did you last arrest anyone? Emil Gruff gets drunk occasionally and Ernst Tigelwurst, the carter, sometimes allow his bullocks to break the three kilometres an hour speed limit. Apart from that, nothing ever happens in Tolokovin. Nobody ever steals anything because nobody has got anything worth stealing." It was Henri Rumboll's turn to pause and allow his eyes to wander, nervously, towards the skylight and the mass of mountain that lay beyond. "There is only one wrong-doer ruining all of our lives . . ." He shivered and then, pulling himself together, clambered to his feet. "Go after him, Sergeant Kropotel. As your mayor, I am telling you that it is your duty. Find the vampire, wherever it is, and kill it. And don't come back to Tolokovin until the vampire lies dead at your feet with a wooden stake through its evil heart."

"It has to be done, Alphonse," said Eric Horowitz. "The mayor is right."

"Very well," said the police sergeant, also clambering to his feet. Then, fixing his gaze on Eric Horowitz, he added, "But I can't manage the task by myself – someone must needs come with me."

"What for?" asked the shopkeeper uneasily,

sensing that he himself was about to be voted into the post of vampire-hunter's assistant.

"I would have thought that that was plainly obvious," replied the police sergeant. "See here," he continued, holding up both his fists. "Imagine that I am holding a wooden mallet in one hand and a sharp-pointed stake in the other."

Eric Horowitz closed his eyes, tight, and tried to imagine such a scene. "Go on," he said at last.

"Do you think that the vampire count is going to stand there quietly while I go to work on him?"

"I don't suppose he is," admitted the shop-keeper, opening his eyes again and shaking his head.

"Of course he isn't! I shall need an assistant – someone to hold down the monster while I do the job."

"You're right, Alphonse," agreed Mayor Rumboll. "Someone must go with you."

"Not me!" replied Eric Horowitz, nervously. Both Alphonse Kropotel and Henri Rumboll were looking straight into his eyes. The thought of having to pin the vampire down on the ground while the police sergeant hammered a stake into its heart sent shivers all along his spine. "Not that I wouldn't jump at the chance of going with you, if only it was possible," he lied. "But what would happen to this village if my shop were to close for any length of time?" Horowitz paused to tap the wooden crate containing the jars of lamp-oil on which he was still sitting, then continued, "Why, every house would be in total darkness when night fell." Then, nodding across at the sacks of chicken-feed, he added, "And what would become of the village's hens if they were forced to go without their food? They would give up laying for a certainty."

"The village store must stay open," murmured Mayor Rumboll, solemnly, aghast at the thought of spending his nights in darkness and his breakfast-times without his usual boiled egg. "Eric Horowitz cannot be spared," he said. "We must think of someone else to act as vampire-hunter's assistant."

"It won't be easy," sighed Sergeant Kropotel. "Only a fool would volunteer to grapple with a vampire."

Eric Horowitz held his silence. But it had occurred to him that, only a moment or so ago, his two companions had been recommending himself for just that position. While Kropotel and Rumboll were considering who they might enlist as the police sergeant's assistant, and while Horowitz was glowering across at his two companions, their thoughts were interrupted by an urgent knocking on the shop door.

"I'll go," said Henri Rumboll, who happened to be standing closest to the storeroom door.

"Tell them we're closed!" called Eric Horowitz as the mayor headed into the shop.

Peering out through the shop door's frosted glass panel, Henri Rumboll could just make out the anxious face of Karl Gustaffe, Tolokovin's baker, peering in at him.

"I need some eggs!" cried the baker, spotting a face behind the glass.

"Can't you read, Gustaffe!" cried Henri

Rumboll through the door, tapping with his forefinger on the CLOSED sign as he spoke. "We're closed."

"But it's Saint Unfortunato's Day next Sunday. I have a score of orders to fill. A feast day's not a feast day without shrubel-cake."

Karl Gustaffe could have saved his breath. He was talking to himself. Mayor Rumboll was already on his way back to the storeroom. He was halfway across the shadowy shop, tip-toeing carefully in order to avoid the many steel-jawed, cheese-baited mousetraps, when an idea occurred to him. He turned, retraced his steps and peered out again through the glass at the baker who was still standing, glumly, on the shop's doorstep.

Henri Rumboll turned the big iron key which grated in the rusting lock. He opened the door and beamed at Karl Gustaffe.

"Come in, Karl!" said the mayor, his smile broadening. "Come through into the storeroom, my dear, good fellow!"

The little baker, wondering what he had done to gain the mayor's approval, stepped through the open doorway into the shop. On many occasions during the days to come, Karl Gustaffe would dearly wish that he had had the good sense to turn down the mayor's invitation and walk away.

"Whoa, Petra!" called the gypsy woman as she tugged gently on the reins. The old horse clip-clopped to a standstill, snorted twice, then shook its head. "So this is where the two of us part company?" said Serafina Krokulengro, turning to her passenger.

"I am more than grateful to you, Serafina, for your kindness in bringing me thus far," said Count Alucard as he clambered down from the green-painted caravan's driving seat. "But you must go where best it suits you, while I am required to choose the opposite route."

The old gypsy and the Transylvanian vampire count had journeyed together along the rutted cart-track for two hours and more. The grey horse, protected from the midday sun by a thick canopy of leaves, had jogged along quite happily between the shafts of the gypsy caravan. They had arrived, at last, at the other side of the forest. Happily, there had been neither sight nor sound of any vampire hunters and Count Alucard had guessed that, by now, the search must have been abandoned. He was relatively safe.

The caravan had pulled up just beyond the fringe of the forest, where the cart-track joined a road. Travelling in one direction, the road meandered off, twisting and turning in leisurely fashion and as far as the eye could see through open countryside. The road's opposite route took a much straighter line and led towards a city which, the count estimated, lay seven or possibly eight kilometres away.

"If you want my advice, Count Alucard, you would be wise to stay well clear of civilisation," said the old woman sharply, frowning as the count peered off towards where the early afternoon sun was glinting on the gold-embellished domes and the glass roofs of the city's taller buildings. "You should take heed from the lesson that your father learned," the gypsy woman continued. "And his father before him. Humankind can only bring you sorrow."

"I know," the Transylvanian nobleman replied with a little sigh. "But all the same I cannot help myself – I feel that my future lies in that direction."

"If you had any sense at all," said Serafina Krokulengro, "you would stay with me and stick to the open road. But there are some people who will never listen to good reason." With which, the old woman flicked at the reins and, with a jerk of its head, the horse started out again, drawing the caravan along the winding road.

"Goodbye, Serafina Krokulengro!" the count called out after the caravan. "And thank you again!"

"Farewell, Count Alucard!" the gypsy woman's voice drifted back. "Good fortune go with thee!"

The count drew back his slim shoulders and set out, taking long strides on his spindly legs, towards the distant city. With luck, he told himself, and if he did not falter in his pace, he should arrive at the city's outskirts before the sun had begun to dip behind the far-off range of hills.

There was another burst of cheering in the market-place and Mayor Henri Rumboll waited for the villagers to fall silent before continuing with the speech that he was making from the steps of the village hall.

"One thing is certain," bellowed the mayor. "You

may be sure that we shall not set eyes again on either of these two brave men until they have brought back the news that the monster which has plagued Tolokovin all these years has been destroyed."

"God protect them both from evil!" cried an old woman dressed in black, who was sitting in the shadows underneath the statue of Saint Unfortunato, busily plucking the feathers from a goose's carcase.

"God go with you, Alphonse Kropotel!" cried several of the villagers while others called out, "God give strength to you too, Karl Gustaffe!" After which, there was another burst of cheering from all across the market-square.

On hearing themselves applauded, the two men who were standing one on either side of the mayor, reacted in different ways. Sergeant Kropotel, wearing his best uniform, his medals and buttons gleaming and his boots well-polished, puffed up with pride as he twirled the ends of his moustache between his fingers and his thumbs. Karl Gustaffe, on the other hand, dressed in the crumpled only suit that he possessed, shuffled his feet on the village-hall steps and chewed nervously at his lower lip.

The village baker was at a total loss to understand why or how he came to be in his present position. Everything had happened so quickly. Only an hour or so ago he had been standing outside Eric Horowitz's shop with nothing more pressing on his mind than calculating the number of shrubel-cakes he might bake in time for Saint

Unfortunato's feast day. Then, out of the blue, Henri Rumboll had invited him into the shop, taken him into the storeroom and, before he knew it, he had somehow been appointed to the post of Official Assistant Vampire Hunter. He had been informed that his duties would entail his accompanying Alphonse Kropotel around the world in search of the Castle Alucard's owner!

How could they ever hope to find Count Alucard, the village baker had asked himself, without so much as a single clue towards his whereabouts? They might search every country around the globe and still not set eyes on their quarry. It could take a lifetime! And supposing they were to find him? What then? He was expected to hold the vampire firmly in his arms while the police sergeant hammered a wooden stake into their captive's heart! Karl Gustaffe grimaced and shivered at the prospect.

"Don't worry, Karl," the mayor had said when the baker had told him that Saint Unfortunato's Day was imminent and that Tolokovin would need his services. "I have a friend who owns a large bakery in the city – we'll get Ernst Tigelwurst to bring in all the shrubel-cakes we need on his bullock-cart."

Which was all very well for Henri Rumboll, the village baker told himself – for the crafty mayor would no doubt sell the city shrubel-cakes at twice the price he had paid for them. And no doubt Ernst Tigelwurst stood to make a handsome profit too in transporting the feast-day cakes. But what was to happen to the village baker's business, while he was trudging around the world, leaving his oven standing idle?

Another chorus of cheers from the villagers brought Karl Gustaffe's thoughts back to the market-square.

"It only remains for me," began Henri Rumboll, holding up his hands for silence, "to present our two brave adventurers with their official tools of office."

As he spoke, Henri Rumboll stooped and picked up a bulky black velvet bag, tied with a gold silken cord, which had been lying at his feet.

The village baker seemed to feel his heart sink down into the pit of his stomach. Karl Gustaffe had recognised instantly (as, indeed, had every person in the square) the bag containing the village's vampire destruction kit: a sturdy wooden mallet and several sharp-pointed wooden stakes.

"Death to the vampire!" shrieked the old crone dressed in black. Her name was Elsa Hoggel and, in her excitement, she had plucked away so frenziedly at the goose's carcase that she was half-hidden in a cloud of tiny goose feathers.

"Death to the vampire!" echoed the voices of the peasants standing shoulder to shoulder in the jam-packed square.

"God speed you on your quest, Alphonse Kropotel," said Mayor Rumboll solemnly as he handed the velvet bag to the police sergeant, adding, "And good fortune to you too, Karl Gustaffe."

"Be sure we shall not come back to Tolokovin," began Sergeant Kropotel, hoisting the velvet bag above his head for all to see, "until a stake from

this velvet bag has been hammered home into the vampire's evil heart!"

The brave words, coupled with that action, drew the loudest cheers of the afternoon. Moments later, the crowd parted in order that Mayor Rumboll could lead the two vampire hunters across the square towards the transport which awaited them.

Ernst Tigelwurst's bullock-cart had been decorated with garlands of wild flowers in honour of the occasion. The carter himself, sitting up on the driving seat, was wearing a sprig of honeysuckle in his hat and there were flowers, too, around the horns of both of the bullocks which were standing, patiently, between the shafts.

"The honour falls to you, Ernst Tigelwurst," the mayor announced importantly, "to convey these gallant heroes on the first leg of their glorious quest!"

"Where are they going?" asked the carter, frowning.

"Anywhere and everywhere! Unceasing in their search until they have sought out and destroyed the evil monster that has plagued this village." Henri Rumboll paused and waved his fist in the air as he added, "To the far corners of the earth, if needs be!"

"I can't go to the far corners of the earth!" the carter muttered to the mayor as the crowd roared its approval at Rumboll's brave words. "I've got a business to run, and a wife and seven children to provide for."

"Take them as far as the city, Ernst," the mayor whispered back. "Drop them off, then call round at Boris Grunwald's bakery – pick up as many shrubel-cakes as he is able to let you have and bring them back here."

"What's in it for me?" growled the carter.

"A share of the handsome profit," hissed Henri Rumboll. "Without any competition, we shall be able to sell the cakes at double their usual price on Saint Unfortunato's Day."

During this whispered conversation, Tolokovin's two vampire hunters had flung the case containing their spare clothing up on to the cart, followed by the bag which held the vampire destruction kit and, finally, had scrambled up themselves. Watched by the village's entire population, Ernst Tigelwurst cracked his whip.

"*Pull*, Osman! *Heave*, Ludwig!" cried the carter to his bullocks.

The two beasts took the strain between them and slowly the cart eased forward, creaking over the cobblestones and then out of the market-square. Alphonse Kropotel and Karl Gustaffe waved their goodbyes at the still cheering villagers and then, as the cart turned a corner, turned to stare at the open road which lay ahead.

Police Sergeant Kropotel, while looking forward keenly to his extended holiday, was also anxious to track down, then destroy the vampire and return to a hero's welcome in Tolokovin. Karl Gustaffe, on the other hand, was in no mood for journeying around the world and wanted to get back to his beloved bakery as soon as possible. At the same time, he had no wish whatsoever to come face-to-face with the vampire count.

As the bullock-cart rumbled on towards the city, the two Tolokovin vampire hunters sat in total silence, each of them lost in his own thoughts.

5

"Tread carefully, Emily," advised Albert Hollins. "Watch where you're putting your feet."

"How can I see where I'm putting my feet, Albert, when I can't see where I'm going?" complained Mrs Hollins, clinging tightly to the back of her husband's jacket. "You told me to keep my eyes shut."

"You can open them now," said Albert Hollins. "You too, Henry."

Henry Hollins, bringing up the rear of the family procession, also with his eyes closed tightly and hanging on to the hem of his mother's fluffy rose-coloured cardigan, blinked as he opened his eyes and took in the back garden.

"Now look around and tell me what you can see that's different," said Albert Hollins.

"Different from what?" asked Emily, puzzled, adding, "What am I supposed to be looking for?"

"If I told you what you were looking for, you wouldn't need to look for it," grumbled Mr Hollins. "What about you, Henry? Can you spot anything you haven't seen before?"

Henry Hollins sighed and shook his head. Still sad about the fact that he was not going to be able to take up his Transylvanian friend's invitation to holiday at Castle Alucard, Henry was not in a mood for playing games. Neither was Emily Hollins disposed towards taking part in Albert's version of "I Spy in the Garden". Emily had left some currant buns browning in the oven and she was fearful that, without an attentive eye kept on them, they would quickly burn.

"Go on, the pair of you," urged Albert Hollins, when neither his wife nor son showed any enthusiasm whatsoever for the diversion he had organised on their behalf. "Get cracking! Use your eyes!"

Realising that they would not be granted any peace until they had spotted a subtle difference in the back garden, Emily and Henry stared all around. There was no doubt in either of their minds that Albert Hollins had introduced another chubby-cheeked, white-bearded garden gnome into the area and that it was their task to identify the newcomer. It was by no means easy-peasy. Wherever Emily and Henry turned their heads, garden gnomes peered back at them, from over every flower-bed, around every bush and shrub and across the garden pond. There were more garden gnomes in the Hollins's back garden than populated the patch of green at the front. Not only that, but every single one of them seemed familiar – it was impossible to tell the interloper.

"I give up," said Emily after a couple of minutes.

"And what about you, Henry?" asked Albert Hollins gleefully. "Do you give up as well?"

Henry Hollins took a very deep breath and then

shook his head. Although he had had no wish, at first, to take any part in his father's gnome-spotting competition, now that he had joined in, he did not want to admit defeat. He screwed up his eyes, turned slowly in a complete circle, peering into every nook and cranny. But, no matter where he looked, it seemed to Henry Hollins that he had seen every gnome before.

"Oh, do give in, Henry," wailed Emily Hollins, thinking desperately about her currant buns.

"All right, Dad," said Henry with a little sigh. "I give up as well."

"There!" exclaimed Albert Hollins triumphantly, pointing upwards over Emily and Henry's heads.

Emily and Henry turned, looking across at where Albert's extended forefinger was indicating. Perched in the fork of a beech tree, some several metres from the ground, a white-bearded, red-coated, green-trousered gnome was peering off towards some distant horizon, his right arm raised to shield his eyes, even though the sun had set some time before.

"That's fooled the both of you," added Albert with a grin.

"That's not fair," said Henry Hollins.

"Garden gnomes don't live in trees," objected Emily.

"That one does," said Albert Hollins. "Or at least he will do as soon as I've built a little tree-house. There wasn't any room for him at ground level." Albert paused and gazed all around the back garden, which was already over-populated with garden gnomes, then added, "And so I had this brilliant idea of housing any new ones overhead. What do you think?"

"I think my currant buns will be burned to a frazzle if I stand here any longer," snapped Mrs Hollins. Turning on her heel, she strode off towards the kitchen door.

"What's your opinion, Henry?" asked Albert. "As I'm not very good at DIY I thought I might buy some little birds' nesting-boxes from the garden centre, paint them red and blue and nail them up there in the branches. Do you think they'd suit as a gnomes' tree-located village?"

Henry Hollins did not reply. The late afternoon was turning into early evening. In the fading light, high in the sky, Henry could just make out a black creature turning on outstretched wing. In his innermost heart, Henry hoped against hope that the flying creature might prove to be his good friend Count Alucard in his vegetarian vampire-bat form, about to swoop down out of the sky and pay the Hollins family a visit. But common sense told Henry that he was gazing up at a common crow; as is usual in such instances, common sense proved to be right.

It had been raining hard, non-stop, for over an hour; the twinkling lights of the Transylvanian city's main-street shop windows were reflected in the widespread puddles which had gathered in the road. Standing in the shadowy doorway which was shared by two separate establishments, Count

Alucard pulled his crimson-lined black cloak up around his ears and shivered. His slim shoulders sagged as he let out a long, sad sigh. On the count's right-hand side was a plain wooden door which led he knew not where, but which had a crack of light spilling out from underneath. It was the contents of the showroom window on his left-hand side which had saddened the Transylvanian nobleman.

Several moments earlier, head down against the driving rain, Count Alucard had taken shelter, only to discover that one half of the doorway he was standing in belonged to a coffin-maker's shop. Staring into the window, the count gazed glumly at the several comfortable coffins on display, their lids propped open. He wondered where he was going to sleep that night. Not in his favourite coffin, in the dungeon back at Alucard Castle, nor his second-best coffin, several countries away across the English Channel, in the sitting-room of his dear friend, Henry Hollins. Even if he were to turn himself into his bat form and fly, day and night, all the way to Staplewood, Count Alucard was too well-mannered to drop in unexpectedly on anyone.

Having taken his leave of the old gypsy woman, Count Alucard had strode for several hours along the country road, arriving on the city's outskirts as the rain began to fall. Getting wetter by the second, he had walked alongside the increasing traffic – horse-drawn carts, ancient motor cars and vintage, single-decker, horn-honking buses, packed with passengers – into the city's centre. It was the time when the shops were closing and both customers and shop assistants alike were headed

homewards, mostly underneath shared umbrellas. They paid scant attention to the gangling, dark-haired, black-cloaked, pointy-toothed, sad-faced fellow loitering on the rainswept pavement.

Now, some thirty minutes later, both shopkeepers and shoppers were gone. In another hour or so, the theatres would open their doors and the restaurants and cafés would be bursting with life but, for the moment at least, it seemed as if Count Alucard had the city entirely to himself.

Taking his wistful gaze away from the comfort of the satin-lined caskets in the coffin-maker's window, the count turned his gaze across the road. Directly opposite was a baker's shop with a mountain of shrubel-cakes piled high in its window and, next door to the baker's, a late-closing greengrocer's with juicy oranges, deep purple fleshy plums and plump, ripe peaches stacked in pyramids on a green-carpeted trestle-table outside on the pavement.

The array of tempting fruit reminded the count that, save for a handful of berries he had plucked from the wayside, he had not eaten all day long. Realising that the rain had stopped at last, he stepped out from the shelter of the doorway in order to get a better view of the mouth-watering display across the road – and was instantly soaked through to the skin.

The heavy wheels of a passing bullock-cart had rumbled through a roadside puddle, sending up a shower of rainwater sufficient to drench the unfortunate count.

"I do wish that you'd look where you are – " the

count began, but he did not complete the sentence. Glancing up, he had instantly recognised not only the bullock-cart and its owner, but also the two men perched beside Ernst Tigelwurst on the driving seat.

The count had seen the cart, and the same two beasts between the shafts, on the countless occasions when Tigelwurst had delivered lamp-oil to the Castle Alucard. Not that the carter had ever dared to make his deliveries to the castle door; Ernst Tigelwurst was too fearful of the vampire legend to even consider such a thing. But Count Alucard had often watched from a castle window as the carter had drawn up outside the castle gates, lowered the oil-drums down to the ground and then driven off, as fast as his lumbering bullocks could take him, back down the winding mountain road that led towards Tolokovin.

It was not, however, the sight of Ernst Tigelwurst and his bullock-cart that had sent shivers racing up and down Count Alucard's spine. Nor was it the presence of Police Sergeant Alphonse Kropotel and Karl Gustaffe, the village baker, sitting next to the carter. No, it was the glimpse he had caught of the bulky, black velvet bag, clutched tightly by the policeman, that had terrified the vegetarian vampire. The count had good reason to recognise Tolokovin's official vampire destruction kit when he set eyes on it. Several of his ancestors had met their end by means of the mallet and sharp-pointed stakes contained within that awful bag.

Hoping against hope that none of the three men on the cart had spotted him, the count shrank back into the shadows in the doorway – but too late, it seemed.

"Look! There!" cried Ernst Tigelwurst, then, "Whoa!"

The urgency in the carter's voice galvanized Count Alucard into action. To the sound of the brake-blocks grating on the cartwheels, the count's long darting fingers found the handle of the coffin-maker's shop door and tugged and pushed at it. But, to his despair, he realised that the door was firmly locked.

Panicking, the Transylvanian vegetarian vampire nobleman turned in the lengthening dark of evening and, thankfully, his long, thin, groping fingers found the second door (which led he knew not where) on the opposite side of the alcove. That door swung open at his touch. There was light beyond. Count Alucard stepped through into a narrow passage. He closed the door behind him, placed his back against it and gave a small sigh of relief. There was no sound of anyone pursuing him and, for the moment at least, he was safe.

Except that he had no idea of the nature of the building he had entered . . .

"What is it?" grumbled Sergeant Kropotel as the wheels of the bullock-cart ground to a final halt. "What have we stopped for?"

"Over *there*!" repeated Ernst Tigelwurst, pointing not towards the shop doorway but over at the opposite side of the road.

"It's a baker's shop!" cried Karl Gustaffe in some

delight and not without a touch of envy, as he looked across at where the carter was pointing.

The shop, which was one of the few still open at that late hour, was much larger and grander than Karl Gustaffe's humble Tolokovin establishment. It also stocked a much wider range of goods. The large double window was filled to overflowing with all manner of Transylvanian delicacies: rancid goat's-cheese tartlets, dried goose-liver profiteroles, sour curd wheat-cakes and other mouth-watering titbits. The name "Boris Grunwald – Master Confectioner" was written in big gold curling letters across the window-pane.

It was the very baker's shop from which Mayor Rumboll had instructed Ernst Tigelwurst to collect shrubel-cakes.

"We haven't got time to stop and stare at cake shops, carter," snarled the police sergeant. "Our business is to do with vampires."

"Then if you seek to pursue that business, Sergeant Kropotel, I suggest that you go about it," replied Ernst Tigelwurst with a shrug of his broad shoulders. "*My* business is to fetch and carry. And my orders were to convey you to this city. Here we are. And this is as far as the pair of you are going on board this waggon."

With which, the carter tethered the two bullocks to a lamp-post and then set off across the road and towards the confectioner's without so much as a backward glance. Sergeant Kropotel and Karl Gustaffe scrambled down on to the pavement and then retrieved their baggage from the back of the cart. Standing in the flickering, pale pool of light cast by the gas-lamp they took in the unfamiliarity of their surroundings and wondered what they should do next. The city was a vast sprawling place of streets and shops and houses. There were a thousand and one places, and more, where a vampire might hide itself . . .

"My dear fellow!" boomed out a voice from behind Count Alucard, causing him to jump. "You are a gift from the gods – a veritable gift from the gods!"

The count, who had been peering backwards through the part-open door to make sure that he was not being followed, turned in the passage to find himself looking up into the piercing eyes of a distinguished-looking gentleman who was even taller than himself.

"I . . . I beg your pardon?" stammered the count.

"No, no, no, my dear good chap!" thundered the man, whose long hair hung over the fur collar of the black overcoat which encased his body. "For it is I who should be begging *your* pardon – humbly and on my knees – for doubting your very existence. But then, I was given to understand that actors were hard to come by in this city."

"I-I-I-I'm afraid that there is some mistake, sir," stuttered the count. "I am not an actor – "

"Come, come, my fine fellow! There is no place in my company for false modesty," boomed the large man, tossing his head so that his long silver locks flew all around his face and then fell back again on to his coat collar. Without warning, he stepped forward, seized Count Alucard in both of

his arms and hugged him warmly. Then, releasing hold, the large man took a backward step and his piercing eyes swept up and down the count, from head to toe and back again. "Excellent! Excellent!" he continued. "Your modesty might have convinced *you* that you are ill-fitted for the part, but I am here to tell you, sirrah, that I could audition a hundred actors and not find one as ideally suited as yourself for this particular role."

In that instant, Count Alucard realised where he was and what had happened. He had trespassed through the stage-door of a theatre. The large man had mistaken him for an actor who was applying for a part in a play.

Being an honest person by nature, the Transylanian vegetarian vampire's first instinct was to tell this gentleman the truth and make his exit. But, if he did so, the count realised that he would find himself outside in the road again – and at the mercy of the vampire hunters. He decided, therefore, that for the moment at least he would continue with the harmless deception, and make his escape after several minutes had elapsed.

"Grantley!" the large man called out along the passage.

"Yes, guv'nor?" The reply came from a stockily-built man with a straggly moustache, wearing a paint-stained brown overall, who had just entered the passage and was studying a notice pinned up on a board.

"Should any other applicants arrive, desirous of auditioning for the butler's role, tell them that the part is already given to Mr . . . er, what did you say your name was, dear fellow?"

"Alucard," replied the count – and then, remembering that he was a hunted man, regretted instantly that he had been so foolish as to give his real name. "Mr C. Alucard," he added quickly, managing to hide the fact, at least, that he was of noble birth.

"Alucard," mused the large man, in rich and fruiy tones. "Alucard?" he said again, and the count held his breath. "Al – U – Card!" the man repeated, this time slowly and allowing the syllables to flow, one by one. "I like the sound of 'Alucard'. It has a goodly ring to it. It is a name that would look good in lights."

The count allowed himself an inward sigh of relief. Clearly, his surname alone meant nothing to the large man – neither did it seem to have any significance for the one in the brown overall. Count Alucard congratulated himself on his good fortune but, at the same time, made a mental note to watch his tongue in future.

"Welcome to the Harcourt Hetherington players, Mr Alucard!" exclaimed the large man, clapping the vegetarian vampire heartily between the shoulder-blades with the palm of a beefy hand. "Grantley will acquaint you with your role this evening. If you will forgive me, I must prepare myself for my own performance. The next time we meet, my dear fellow, it shall be upon the stage!" With which, and with a flourish of his hand above his head, the large man strode off along the passage and towards his dressing-room, calling out the count's name yet again, "Al – U – Card!" And then, glancing back over his shoulder, he added, "It is an actor's name if ever I heard one." With a final wave of his hand, he disappeared around a corner.

"Who is he?" asked Count Alucard, impressed by the large man's proud and upright bearing. "Is he somebody important?"

"Who *is* he!" echoed the man called Grantley, in scoffing disbelief. "Why, he's the guv'nor, he is! He's Mr Harcourt Hetherington, the world-famous actor. I'll say he's important – not half, he isn't! He's the most important person you're ever likely to come across! Call yourself an actor, and you've never heard of Mr Harcourt Hetherington?"

"To be absolutely frank with you, I *don't* call myself an actor," replied the count, deciding to take the brown-overalled man into his confidence – in part, at least. For one thing, he had just lied to Harcourt Hetherington and his natural honesty forbade him from telling one lie after another. And for another thing, the man called Grantley had a friendly face behind his big moustache. He seemed like someone the count could put his trust in. "To tell you the absolute honest truth," he continued, "I have never acted upon the stage in my entire life."

"Then why did you apply for the butler's part in the play we're doing?"

"But I didn't."

"Yes, you did," insisted the brown-overalled man, nodding at the count's clothing. "You even came dressed up in a butler's costume."

"These are the clothes I always wear," said Count Alucard, glancing down at his black suit, white starched shirt and white bow-tie. There were times when his formal manner of dress seemed to cause nothing but problems. "As a matter of fact, I came in through that door to hide from a couple of men who wish to kill me."

"Why, what have you done?" The brown-overalled man's eyes widened and his moustache trembled as he added, "Did you kill somebody first?"

"Of course not!" replied Count Alucard, stoutly. "I wouldn't dream of it. I wouldn't harm a living thing – I *couldn't*." His slim shoulders drooped despondently as he continued, "It's all a foolish misunderstanding. But I mustn't take up any more of your valuable time with my problems. I imagine that my pursuers will have gone by now and so, if you'll accept my heartfelt apologies for having put yourself and Mr Hetherington to so much trouble, I'll be on my way."

Then, giving a polite but grave little bow by

way of taking his leave, Count Alucard moved back along the passage towards the door through which he had entered. Just to assure himself that the coast *was* clear, he opened it gently, peered through the narrow gap – then closed the door with a gulp.

"Oh, dear!" he murmured. "Oh, heavens above!"

"Are they still there?"

Count Alucard nodded glumly, his shoulders drooping even further. His split-second glance through the part-open door had been sufficient for him to see not only Sergeant Kropotel and Karl Gustaffe standing with their backs to him, but also the bulky black velvet bag tucked under the police sergeant's arm, containing the vampire destruction kit. Even worse, the count had also seen that it had begun to rain, heavily – the two Tolokovinite vampire hunters had taken shelter in the doorway. If the rain continued, they could be standing there for *hours*!

"I don't suppose, by any chance, that there's another way out of here?" he quavered.

"There is, but – "

"Is there *really*?" broke in the count, his face aglow with sudden hope.

"I hadn't finished. I was about to say: I *could* take you through the pass-door, into the auditorium, across the foyer, past the box-office and out into the street through the front entrance of the theatre – "

"That would be extremely kind of you," the count broke in for a second time.

"But supposing I did? How do you know there

won't be more men waiting for you there as well as those outside the stage-door?"

"Surely not?" The count's pale face crumpled at the prospect.

"It's possible," said the man called Grantley, finding it hard not to smile at the way in which the count's mood changed in an instant from despair to hope, and back again. "Besides, supposing you did manage to give the slip to these men who are chasing you – where would you go? Have you got any money?"

"Not at this particular moment in time," the count admitted. "Not on my person."

"Then it seems to me that we are in a position to help each other – you need employment and a place to rest your head, we are in dire need of someone to play the butler's part in the play tonight. You – " The man paused and waved his hand at Count Alucard's clothing, then continued, "would seem ideally suited to take on that role."

"But I've already told you," said the count, sighing again, "I am not an actor. Besides, even if I were, there is no way that I could learn the words the butler has to say in time for tonight's performance."

"Don't worry – that's the last thing that need concern you," said the man, giving a little chuckle. Then, extending his hand, he went on, "I'm Grantley, by the by. Grantley Hardcastle. I'm the stage-manager. Come along, Mr Alucard, I'll show you to your dressing-room."

Count Alucard hesitated for a moment, unsure of what he should do. He was required to choose, he told himself, between the fire and the frying-pan. He could either go out in front of an audience and attempt to play a part of which he did not know a single line; or he could venture into the night and fall foul of the two Tolokovinite vampire hunters whose sole intentions were to destroy him. The count gave a little gulp as he recalled the contents of the black bulky bag the two men carried with them. It did not take much longer than a second for Count Alucard to make up his mind.

"Do you promise me I won't have *too* many words to learn?" he murmured anxiously as he allowed Grantley Hardcastle to lead him along the passage and into the back-stage area of the theatre.

The stage-manager made no reply but, instead, glanced up into the vegetarian vampire's eyes, winked and smiled a little smile.

6

"'Dinner is served, milord'?" said Count Alucard, with a slightly puzzled frown.

"That's right," replied Grantley Hardcastle, with a nod.

The stage-manager and the vegetarian vampire were standing on the theatre's stage, which was set with the scenery, furniture and props for Act One of *Murder At Maltravers Hall*, the play which the Hetherington Players were to perform that evening. A single light shone down on the library set. The curtain had been raised, the lights were on in the auditorium, and the count could not help but feel a tingle of excitement as he gazed out across the row upon row of empty seats, soon to be filled with eager Transylvanian theatre-goers. The stage-manager had told him that the performance was a sell-out. Although the vampire count had not, at first, been keen to become an actor, the very act of walking out on to the stage had fired his enthusiasm. There was a little bit of the show-off in Count Alucard (if ever he had the opportunity) and he was bursting with enthusiasm to play the part he had been given. He was a trifle disappointed now at discovering that there wasn't very much of a part for him to play.

" 'Dinner is served, milord'?" Count Alucard repeated the words. "Is that the only line I've got to say?" he could not hide his disappointment.

"That's right," the stage-manager said again, going on to explain, "Those are the very first words spoken in the play. Then, when Lord Maltravers – that's the role Mr Hetherington portrays – when he says, 'Thank you, Carstairs,' you bow, turn, carrying your butler's silver tray, and go off through that door over there."

"And don't I come back on again?"

"Not in the first act, no," replied Grantley Hardcastle. The stage-manager frowned, stooped, then picked up a toffee-wrapper which some careless stage-hand had dropped on the library carpet. He slipped the scrap of paper into his overall pocket, before continuing, "But you are on stage throughout the entire second act."

"Am I?" exclaimed the count, perking up. "And do I have a great many lines to say in the second half of the play?"

"None at all," said Grantley Hardcastle, with a firm shake of his head. "You're dead."

"Dead?"

"As yesterday's cold mutton. When the second act curtain rises, you are discovered stretched out on the drawing-room floor, with an ornate Oriental dagger in your back."

"Oh, dear!" Count Alucard's slim shoulders drooped despondently. "Is that all that I have to do – just lie there?"

"*All?*" Grantley Hardcastle's voice rose crossly, and his eyebrows furrowed and touched each other above his nose. "I know that you're just a beginner, Mr Alucard, but – believe you me – you have a great deal to learn about the acting profession!"

"I shall do my very best to be a willing pupil."

"To begin with, then, you must understand that playing the role of the dead body in a murder play is not the easiest of tasks – as you shall discover for yourself before the night is over."

"Why not?" enquired the count. "Don't I just lie there, on the carpet, and keep quite still?"

"You'll find out," replied the stage-manager grimly. "The first few minutes aren't so bad, but just you wait until you've been stretched out on that stage for a quarter of an hour, without being able to move so much as a single muscle, and your nose begins to itch . . ."

"How do you know that my nose will start to itch?"

"Because that's what always happens," said Grantley Hardcastle. "I've known scores of actors who have had to play dead bodies, in one play or another, and I've never come across one yet that didn't suffer from the dreaded itchy-nose. Come on, I'll show you to your dressing-room." With which, the stage-manager turned and led the way backstage. "By the way," he called over his shoulder to Count Alucard, who was following close behind him, "before I take my leave of you, would you like me to hear your words again – the ones you say at the beginning of Act One?"

The count, his thoughts concerned with how he might cope if he were to suffer the "dreaded itchy-nose" while he was lying still on stage, was forced to make another confession. "I – I'm afraid I can't quite bring to mind what it is I'm supposed to say. . . ."

"Surely you haven't forgotten your line already!" groaned Grantley Hardcastle. " 'Dinner is served, milord,' " he reminded the vegetarian vampire, pausing in the backstage corridor where the dressing-rooms were located.

" 'Dinner is served, milord,' " repeated the count, then added, "I'll remember."

"Be sure you do – or else there will be trouble," said the stage-manager. Then, opening the door to a tiny room, he added, "This is your dressing-room."

The room, which was no larger than a cubby-hole, had space only for a rickety chair, which stood in front of an equally rickety dressing-table, on which there were some stubs of sticks of grease-paint contained in an old cigar-box and discarded by the previous actor-occupier.

"They'll come in useful!" the count murmured to himself, for he knew that if he were to appear in a play on stage, he would need to put some colour into his vampirical pale complexion. But his delight at spotting the odds and ends of make-up quickly dissolved as soon as his eyes took in the large mirror, surrounded by electric light bulbs, which was fastened to the wall above the table. "Oh, my goodness me!" Count Alucard murmured

to himself. "That's sure to provide me with some problems . . ."

"What's the matter?" asked Grantley Hardcastle. He had not heard the words that the vegetarian vampire had muttered under his breath, but he could not help but notice the look of horror that had crossed his face. "Is something wrong?"

"N-n-n-no – not a thing," replied the count, quickly recovering his composure. Then, stepping through the door, he called back over his shoulder, "If you'll excuse me, Mr Hardcastle – I must go over my line again!" With which, he quickly closed the door behind him, leaving the stage-manager outside in the passage.

The vegetarian vampire slumped down on to the chair, his shoulders drooping, and gazed glumly into the mirror. He saw the room, the chair and table reflected in the glass – everything except himself. Vampires, as every Transylvanian child is taught at school, do not possess a reflection. It was this fact, and the presence of the mirror, which caused the count's concern. If he should be joined in the tiny dressing-room by any other person, the absence of his reflection in the mirror would reveal his true identity immediately. The stage-manager had been kind enough to come to the count's rescue earlier that evening, helping him to evade his pursuers, but Count Alucard knew that he could not expect the same kind of assistance were he to be exposed as a real-life vampire.

"Oh, what a miserable life is mine," groaned Count Alucard, overcome for the moment with self-pity.

"Steady, Osman! . . . Gently, Ludwig!" Ernst Tigelwurst murmured into his bullocks' ears, stroking the tufted hair between their horns. His wooden cart was parked at the back of Boris Grunwald's smart confectionery shop, and the carter was worried that his animals might take fright at all the activity which was going on. Several of the shop's girl assistants, neatly uniformed in black dresses, white aprons and matching white mob caps, were scurrying to and fro, carrying bulging brown-paper carrier bags from out of the shop's back door and piling them on to the rear of the cart.

"Forty-five . . . forty-six . . ." grunted Boris Grunwald, the red-cheeked, portly confectioner, carefully counting each carrier bag and then entering it, in pencil, in his big order-book. "Forty-seven . . . forty-eight . . ."

Ernst Tigelwurst blew out his cheeks as the carrier bags kept on coming. He wondered how many shrubel-cakes were contained inside each carrier bag. And how much money Mayor Rumboll would make when he resold them, at a profit, in Tolokovin.

"... forty-nine.... fifty!" cried the confectioner, entering that total in the order-book and then proffering it to the carter, together with the stub of a pencil. "There are five paper bags inside every one of those carriers, and each paper bag holds four shrubel-cakes. That's a thousand shrubel-cakes in all." Without knowing it, Boris Grunwald had answered the first part of the question that Ernst Tigelwurst had put to himself. "Tell Henri Rumboll that's as many as I can spare him – it's Saint Unfortunato's day here next Sunday, as well as in Tolokovin. And I'll thank you for your signature at the bottom of the page."

The carter frowned, both at the order-book and at the pencil, before making a confession. "I can't read or write – I never learned," he said, before adding, "But I can put an X."

"An X will suit admirably," said Boris Grunwald, but to himself he murmured, "Heavens above! These Tolokovinite villagers are as thick as pine-trees!" Then, aloud, he said, "Tell Henri Rumboll I will post the bill on to him in a day or two."

Ernst Tigelwurst took both order-book and pencil, then slowly and carefully inscribed an X at the place on the page where the confectioner had indicated. He paused after he had made his mark, drew back his head and gazed at his handiwork in admiration. The carter might not have ever studied hard enough in school to have learned the skill of forming all the letters of the alphabet, but he had been signing his name in this manner for a great many years, and was proud of his ability to set down an X. A moment later, he was back up on the driving seat. With a crack from the whip above their heads, Osman and Ludwig tugged hard in the shafts and the cartwheels lumbered forward.

"A thousand shrubel-cakes!" mused Ernst Tigelwurst, as the bullock-cart moved out from the rear of the confectionery shop and into the rain-glistening main shopping street. "Mayor Rumboll will surely make a fortune!" the carter told himself. There was not a single Tolokovinite – man, woman or child – who would not want a shrubel-cake on Saint Unfortunato's Day. "He will sell every single one of them, and at a handsome profit. Why, if he pays a grubeck each for the shrubel-cakes, then sells them for a grubeck and a half, he will have earned himself . . ." But the carter never came up with the answer to that problem; as well as being unable to read or write, Ernst Tigelwurst had never paid much attention during his arithmetic lessons either.

Struggling with the teaser in his head, Tigelwurst failed to notice the two men, both of them wet and cold, standing outside the entrance to the theatre on the opposite side of the street. Had he done so, he would have recognised Karl Gustaffe and Alphonse Kropotel, the two vampire hunters he had dropped off a little earlier that evening. Not that he would have had much to say to either of those gentlemen, who, in their turn, would have had few good words to say about the man who had left them standing in the rain.

"Gee up, Osman! Step smartly, Ludwig!" Dismissing the mayor's money-making shrubel-cake scheme from his mind, Ernst Tigelwurst gave two quick cracks with his long whip over the bullocks' heads, and the two huge animals picked up their lumbering pace. The rain was sheeting down again. Osman and Ludwig, sensing that they were homeward bound, made better speed. With luck, the carter told himself, he would sleep safe and sound that night, tucked up in his own bed in the loft above the bullocks' byre, comforted by the familiar smells and warmed by the steam that rose up from the straw and animals below him.

"Are you mad, Karl Gustaffe?" snarled Police Sergeant Kropotel, shaking himself like a wet puppy until his medals rattled, in order to rid his uniform of the excess rain. "There is an evil, blood-drinking vampire at large, roaming this city, and you suggest that we spend the evening watching a *play*? Have you completely lost possession of your senses?"

"Do you have a better suggestion?" replied the baker, wearily. Karl Gustaffe was also soaked through to the skin. He tried, without success, to find shelter from the driving rain by hugging the wall beneath the narrow ornate canopy above the theatre's entrance.

"I do indeed!" declared Kropotel. He raised the

sopping wet black velvet bag containing the hammer and stakes above his head and shook it, as he continued, "To finish off the task that we have vowed to complete! To seek, to find, and then to finish off the hideous blood-sucking monster!"

"Well spoken, Sergeant," replied the baker, sarcastically. "Except that we haven't got the faintest idea where to begin to look. The vampire could be anywhere – you've admitted that fact yourself. We haven't a hope in heaven of even catching sight of it. The only thing we look like catching is our death of cold." Then, as if to emphasise the truth of this statement, Karl Gustaffe sneezed, very loudly, twice: "Ah-*choo*! AH-*chooo*!"

Police Sergeant Kropotel did not reply immediately. His wet clothing clinging uncomfortably to his skin, he realised the truth in what his companion had said. Also, at that moment, there were signs of life from inside the theatre. Someone had switched on the foyer lights, casting a rosy, inviting glow through the frosted glass panels in the locked front doors. An evening spent sitting in a comfortable theatre seat would certainly be preferable to one spent trudging rainy streets on a hopeless quest.

"What's the play that's on in there tonight?" ventured the police sergeant.

In answer, Karl Gustaffe nodded at the poster which was pasted on the wall:

The Harcourt Hetherington Players
proudly present:
Mr HARCOURT HETHERINGTON
and Company
in
MURDER AT MALTRAVERS HALL
A Mystery Play
directed by
Harcourt Hetherington

There was a strip of paper, stuck across the poster, which read: **FINAL PERFORMANCE AT THIS THEATRE!**

"I haven't been inside a theatre for years and years," said the police sergeant wistfully. "Or to any other kind of entertainment. There isn't time for that sort of thing when you're a policeman. My parents used to take me to the travelling circus when I was a little boy."

"I used to go there too!" said Karl Gustaffe, excitedly. "Every time the circus came to Tolokovin. I wanted to be a clown when I grew up."

"I always wanted to be the ringmaster, so that I could crack the whip and make everyone obey my orders."

You haven't changed much, Sergeant Kropotel! said the baker to himself, but he didn't dare to voice his thoughts aloud. Instead, he took two paces quickly to the right, as a gutter overflowed in the canopy above his head, sending a stream of cold rainwater down the back of his neck.

It was at this point that a coach, drawn by a

single horse, pulled up outside the theatre. Simultaneously, the entrance doors were opened and a red-coated commissionaire hurried out, opening a large umbrella and brushing the vampire hunters aside. The commissionaire shepherded the coach's passengers – a grey-haired man with a beaky nose and a rather large lady wearing a ballgown – into the theatre without either of them suffering a single drop of rain. Before the doors swung shut again, Alphonse Kropotel felt a warm draught of air from inside the foyer, bringing with it the smell of coffee and the sounds of a violin and a saxophone tuning up in the orchestra pit.

"We have to begin our vampire hunt somewhere," began the police sergeant, slowly, "so we could start the search inside this theatre."

"What a good idea, Sergeant!" replied Karl Gustaffe.

Both the police sergeant and his assistant knew that there was not the slightest chance of them coming across the vampire in the theatre, but it gave them a good excuse for getting out of the rain.

"Jump to it, Gustaffe!" snapped Sergeant Kropotel to his assistant. Once the policeman had made his mind up on any matter, he was a man of action. Besides, he was now so wet that the ends of his military-style moustache – which normally pointed upwards, needle-sharp, on either side of his nostrils – were drooping downwards, bedraggled, over the corners of his mouth. "Pick up that luggage!" he continued, nodding at the suitcase on the pavement. "Let's get indoors!"

Karl Gustaffe did not need a second invitation.

Carrying the case which contained all their clean clothing, he hastened into the welcoming warmth of the theatre foyer, followed by Alphonse Kropotel, who was clutching the black velvet bag which held the famous vampire destruction kit of Tolokovin.

"Come in!" called Count Alucard, in answer to the brisk rapping on his dressing-room door. Then, as soon as the words were out of his mouth, he dropped down on to the floor, on hands and knees.

"'Tis only I, dear friend, come to wish you well on your debut perfor – " began Harcourt Hetherington, peering round the door, dressed in his Lord Maltravers costume. But he broke off in some concern at the sight of the newest recruit to his theatrical company scrabbling on the dressing-room floor. "Is something amiss?" he added, blinking in surprise.

"Not at all, sir," the count hastened to assure his employer. "Except that I appear to have mislaid my dressing-room key – and I wondered if it might have fallen on the floor – and so I got down on my hands and knees to look for it." Count Alucard had kept his pale, slim fingers crossed while he said these words, for he was not telling the truth. The plain fact of the matter, of course, was that the vegetarian vampire was afraid of being discovered without a reflection in the big illuminated mirror over his dressing-table, and thus giving away his true identity.

"Never fear," said the old actor. "I'm sure your

key will turn up somewhere. Meanwhile, concern yourself with more important matters. Have you managed to master the butler's role to your satisfaction? In short – have you learned your line?"

" 'Dinner is served, milord!' " replied the count immediately, from underneath the dressing-table. He had rattled off his only speech so many times inside his head that he felt sure he would be able to say it in his sleep.

"Word perfect, congratulations!" cried Harcourt Hetherington, making a fist and punching at the air above his head. "The next time that you and I meet, sirrah, will be upon the stage!" The actor gave the vegetarian vampire a cheery wave, turned on his heel and left, closing the door behind him.

Count Alucard waited until the actor's footsteps had faded along the passage, before crawling out from underneath his dressing-table. Clambering to his feet, the Transylvanian nobleman gazed thoughtfully into the mirror – at the reflection of the three walls of the empty room.

"*Oompah, oompah-pah . . .*" His cheeks puffed out, three strands of hair plastered down over his otherwise bald head, the fat musician blew hard into his euphonium in the theatre's orchestra-pit. The violinist and the saxophonist waited, their instruments at the ready, until their companion had finished his solo, and then joined in. At the same time, the huge, twinkling chandelier which hung above the audience gradually dimmed.

"Here goes, Sergeant," breathed Karl Gustaffe,

shuffling his bottom excitedly in his faded red plush seat in the stalls. "It's going to begin!"

"Hush!" went the police sergeant grimly. Alphonse Kropotel knew that he would not enjoy the play one little bit if Karl Gustaffe was going to spend the entire evening whispering and wriggling in his seat. "And do try to keep *still*."

"Sorry, Sergeant." But the village baker was far too excited at the prospect of the night ahead to be able to obey his comrade's commands. Continuing to wriggle his behind, he swivelled his head this way and that, as he took in the splendour of the darkening theatre: the ornate gilded plasterwork that decorated the front of the circle, the painted cherubs dancing on the ceiling. Karl Gustaffe twisted and turned so much, in fact, that he dislodged the bulky black velvet bag that was resting, for safe-keeping, on Alphonse Kropotel's knees. The wooden mallet and the sharp-pointed stakes rattled together noisily as the bag fell on the wooden floor.

"You clumsy oaf, Gustaffe!" snarled Sergeant Kropotel.

"Sorry, Sergeant!"

As one, the two vampire hunters bent forward to retrieve the precious vampire destruction kit. *Crack*! The sound of their heads banging together echoed through the auditorium.

"Ouch!" went Alphonse Kropotel.

"Oooh!" went Karl Gustaffe.

Their cries of pain were drowned in the burst of applause that came from the audience as the house-lights dimmed completely. The heavy red curtain rose on *Murder At Maltravers Hall*, Act One, Scene One: The Library.

Lord Maltravers, played by Harcourt Hetherington elegantly got up in evening dress, was posed by a part of the scenery which was painted to look like a bookcase full of leather-bound books. Lady Maltravers, a part taken by the well-known actress, Fiona Carlton-Walters (Mrs Harcourt Hetherington in real life), wearing a long blue gown and a tiara twinkling with stage-diamonds, was standing stock still at her husband's side. Another actress, a pretty girl, eighteen years of age, cast in the role of Lord and Lady Maltravers' daughter, the Honourable Anthea Maltravers (and whose real name was Lucy Lanebury), was poised dramatically on the edge of the library chair. Yet another member of that theatrical company in the part of Sir Archie Granville, the Maltravers' house-guest, wearing a loud check suit, a false moustache, and a gold watch-chain hanging acros his waistcoat front (and whose real name was Bernard Dugdale) was standing in front of the painted library fireplace, holding a newspaper.

These four held their breath as they stared across at Carstairs, the Maltravers' butler (Count Alucard, of course), who was standing, tray in hand, framed in the library doorway. They waited, on tenterhooks, for Carstairs to deliver the play's opening words.

Count Alucard gulped, not once but twice; no matter how hard he tried, he was unable to stop the tray shaking in his hands. Looking past the glare of the footlights, he could see nothing but

blackness – all the same, he was aware of the audience that was out there, also waiting for him to break the silence. Alas, he was unable to perform that task. He had quite forgotten what it was that he had to say. Which was ridiculous. Only a moment ago, before the curtain had gone up, he had had his line off perfectly, inside his head. He had said it to himself, with confidence, a hundred times inside his dressing-room. But now, standing here on the stage, his mind was a total blank. His mouth opened and closed several times, but not a single sound came out.

The Transylvanian vegetarian vampire count turned actor was going through that agony which, sooner or later, is suffered by all members of the theatrical profession: Count Alucard was suffering from a bad attack of stage-fright. Shaking now from head to foot, his mouth still opening and closing soundlessly, he prayed that a trapdoor might accidentally open on the stage and, mercifully, swallow him down whole. No such luck.

Thankfully, there was one person present who was capable of saving the situation. Harcourt Hetherington, that seasoned old theatrical campaigner, had experienced similar situations with other despairing actors on stages all around the world. Clearing his throat, then glancing round at his fellow actors, he made up a speech on the spur of the moment to jog Count Alucard's memory.

"I imagine, Carstairs," said the old actor, in his Lord Maltravers voice, "that dinner is most probably served?"

"Dinner *is* served, milord," replied the count.

Harcourt Hetherington's timely intervention had done the trick. Having managed to say his line at last, Count Alucard turned and stumbled off into the wings.

The actors left behind in the library all breathed a sigh of relief.

"Before we go in for dinner, Lord Maltravers," said Sir Archie Granville, taking his gold watch out of his waistcoat pocket, "the time has come for me to tell you something that I think you ought to know . . ."

That night's performance of *Murder At Maltravers Hall* was up and running and back on course.

7

If the vampire hunters of Tolokovin had been paying attention when the curtain rose on *Murder At Maltravers Hall*, they would have surely spotted the vampire they had been ordered to seek out and destroy in front of their very eyes, performing the butler's role in the play which they had paid two grubecks each to see. In which circumstance, they would have raced up on to the stage, taken the dreaded vampire into custody and removed him from the theatre. Later that same night, they would have done their duty and hammered a sharp wooden stake through the poor unfortunate monster's heart. And that would have been the end of this particular Transylvanian tale.

Fortunately, as things turned out, Alphonse Kropotel and Karl Gustaffe had chanced to crack their heads together at the very same moment as the play began. Dazed by this minor accident, the police sergeant and his baker assistant had spent over thirty seconds scrabbling on the floor beneath their seats, searching for the wooden stakes and the mallet, which had tumbled out of the black velvet bag as it hit the floorboards. And that was the all-important half a minute taken up by Count

Alucard striving, inside his head, for the words he had to say.

With the vampire destruction kit stowed back in its bag, Kropotel and Gustaffe, still rubbing ruefully at their heads, struggled back into their seats at the very moment that the count turned on his heel and strode backstage and out of sight.

"Before we go in for dinner, Lord Maltravers," said Sir Archie Granville, taking his gold watch out of his waistcoat pocket, "the time has come for me to tell you something that I think you ought to know . . ."

Alphonse Kropotel was at last now able to turn his attention to what was happening on the stage. Being a policeman, he looked forward to seeing a play which had a murder in it. It would be just up his street! Kropotel had decided that he would try to guess which one of the characters was going to get killed – and then, afterwards, he would work out which one of them had done it. Karl Gustaffe was equally excited. He was not concerned with what the play was about, just thrilled at being in the theatre. Squirming in his seat, the baker rolled his programme into a tube, squinted through it as if it was a telescope, then unrolled it back to its original shape.

"Stop making rustling noises with that programme," hissed Sergeant Kropotel. "And do stop fidgeting, Gustaffe. I'm trying to concentrate."

"Sorry, Sergeant," replied the baker.

"I'm sorry, Mr Hardcastle," murmured Count

Alucard, blinking up at the stage-manager from underneath the dressing-table. "I was so sure I knew my words when I went on to the stage, but as soon as the curtain rose, my mind was a total blank."

The curtain had just fallen on the first act of *Murder At Maltravers Hall* and, finding himself with a moment to spare, Grantley Hardcastle had hurried down to see Count Alucard. To his surprise, the stage-manager had found the actor on the floor of his dressing-room.

"And so you should be sorry," scolded Mr Hardcastle. "Mr Hetherington is extremely angry, I don't mind telling you. And what are you doing down there?" he added, puzzled.

"I appear to have mislaid my dressing-room key," said Count Alucard, using the same fib that he had tried out earlier that evening. "I wondered whether it might, perhaps, have fallen underneath the table."

"There are more important things things in life than dressing-room keys!" snapped Grantley Hardcastle. "If you *really* want to be an actor – "

"Oh, I do! I do!" broke in the count.

" – Then the one thing that you must understand is that the play comes first – above *all else*! You've made a mess of the first act, and you only had one line to learn. Now you have to go out there, in front of that audience, for a whole hour."

"At least I haven't got any words to say in the second act," said the vegetarian vampire, nervously running his slim, pale fingers through his long black hair. "I only have to lie very still."

"How many times do I have to tell you that it isn't easy, playing the part of a dead body?"

"I know," said the count. "I haven't forgotten about the 'dreaded itchy-nose'."

"The curtain goes up again in ten minutes' time. If I were you, I'd stretch myself out while I had the opportunity and rehearse my role."

"You're right, Mr Hardcastle," agreed the count, spreading his long legs across the floor. "And that's exactly what I intend to do."

"Oh – before I go . . ." The stage-manager paused, took a slip of paper from out of his overall pocket and handed it to the count. "There wasn't time, of course, to have your name printed inside the programme for tonight's performance, but we did manage to get these run off in the theatre office. The usherettes put them into all of the programmes – just thought that you might like to know. I'll leave you to get on with the good work," he said. Then, as he stepped over the count's gangly body which was sprawled across the floor, he added, "Break a leg!"

"I beg your pardon?" the count said, puzzled.

"Break a leg," the stage-manager repeated. "It's a saying that we have in the theatre. It means 'Good luck'."

"Well, I never!" said Count Alucard. As the door closed behind Grantley Hardcastle, the vegetarian vampire murmured to himself, "One lives and learns . . ." Holding the slip of paper up to the light, he studied the printed wording.

IMPORTANT NOTICE
Cast Alteration
At tonight's performance, the part of
CARSTAIRS, THE BUTLER
will be portrayed by:
Mr C. ALUCARD, Esq.

The vegetarian vampire stared at the words long and hard, and with mixed feelings. He was proud to see his family name in print and associated with the theatrical profession, rather than on a "Wanted" poster with a reward for his capture, alive or dead. But another small voice inside his head reminded him that, considering he was trying to evade the two Tolokovin vampire hunters, it might have been better if he could have played the butler's role in *Murder At Maltravers Hall* without any publicity whatsoever.

Although I don't suppose it really matters, the count told himself. Sergeant Kropotel and Karl Gustaffe are going to be far too busy searching the city streets for me. They're hardly likely to be sitting out there in the audience.

"For the last time, Gustaffe," growled Sergeant Kropotel, "stop fiddling with that programme!" To pass the time during the interval, the baker had returned to rolling up the programme and peering through it, telescope-fashion; this time at the well-to-do people in the front row of the circle. "And pass it over here," the policeman added, "I'd like to have a read of that myself, when you've finished messing it about."

"Sorry, Sergeant." Karl Gustaffe unrolled the theatre programme and tried to smooth it back to its original condition. "Which one is it, do you think, that's going to get murdered?" he asked, trying to turn the policeman's mind to other matters.

Alphonse Kropotel rubbed hard at the dark stubble on his chin and gave the question his consideration. The first act of *Murder At Maltravers Hall* had consisted, mostly, of bitter accusations and fierce arguments between the characters on the stage. Every single one of them, or so it seemed, had some good reason for wanting somebody or other dead. But the curtain had fallen for the interval with all of them still on their feet and in the best of health, without a clue as to which one would be the victim.

"Let's see now," the policeman said at last, "I haven't quite worked out yet which one of them is going to die . . ." He paused, and then continued with a knowing smile, " . . . but I *can* tell you which one of them will be the murderer."

"Who?"

"It'll be the butler," said Kropotel, with a shrug.

"What makes you think that?"

"It always *is* the butler who does the dirty deed in murder mysteries. I haven't been a policeman all these years without learning that much. I'll wager you a grubeck that the butler does it."

"But we don't even know that there's a butler in the play," argued the baker. Which was true – when

Carstairs had made his brief entrance at the beginning of the play, both Kropotel and Gustaffe, dazed after their collision of heads, had been scrabbling on the floor beneath their seats, recovering the precious contents of the black velvet bag.

"There's *always* a butler in a murder play – and it's *always* him that's the guilty party," the police sergeant replied, impatiently. "And if you'll be so kind as to hand me that programme, as I asked, I'll tell you the name of the actor who is playing the butler."

By this time, having rolled the pages several times in the opposite direction, Karl Gustaffe had succeeded in turning his paper spyglass back into a theatre programme. He handed it over meekly to the policeman.

"About time too!" snapped Alphonse Kropotel, turning to the centre pages where the characters in the play were listed. "Hello! What have we here?" he continued, as he came across the printed piece of paper tucked inside the middle of the programme. But at the very moment that Kropotel peered at the slip of paper, the auditorium lights began to dim. It was impossible for him to read the printed information. The policeman put the paper back inside the programme for safe-keeping and turned all his attention to the stage.

"Here we go again!" exclaimed Karl Gustaffe in excitement as the rich red curtain, trimmed with gold, began to rise.

Here we go again! Count Alucard told himself as

he lay motionless on the stage and watched the curtain begin to rise. If only my nose doesn't start to itch, I should be able to hold this position without moving, he told himself. And even if I *do* get an itchy nose, I shall do my very utmost not to scratch it.

The vegetarian vampire was determined to succeed. By forgetting his words at the beginning of the play, he realised that he had not only let himself down but also, more importantly, his fellow actors. He meant to make up for his first act misdemeanours by performing the role of the dead body in the second half to absolute perfection. As the heavy curtain rose on its pulleys and disappeared into the blackness overhead, the count stiffened his limbs and prepared himself to move not so much as a muscle.

The second act of *Murder At Maltravers Hall* was set in the Maltravers' drawing-room and, when the curtain went up, it was on a darkened stage with the butler's dead body stretched out on the carpet. A moment later, the count knew, Lord Maltravers (played by Harcourt Hetherington) would enter, switch on the lights, and the butler's body would be revealed for all to see.

It was in those final moments, as the lights dimmed over the audience and while the stage was still in complete darkness, that Count Alucard got the biggest shock of that day. Stretched out on the drawing-room carpet, looking out across the still darkened footlights, the vegetarian vampire's sharp eyes fastened on two all too familiar faces. Karl Gustaffe, the Tolokovin baker, and Alphonse Kropotel, Tolokovin's sergeant of police, were sitting side-by-side in the third row of the stalls, and looking straight towards him. But what caused the vampire's heart to beat all the faster was the sight of the bulging black velvet bag balanced on the policeman's lap.

And it was not only Count Alucard's heart that was racing faster than usual – his thoughts were spinning round in his head at an incredible pace. He wondered, wildly, what he ought to do. His first instinct was to leap to his feet while the stage was still in darkness, and rely on his long legs to return him to the road outside before anyone in the theatre company had realised that he was gone, or either of the vampire hunters had even been aware that he was present. But a wiser voice inside his head advised him not to behave so rashly.

Karl Gustaffe and Alphonse Kropotel could not know that he was in the play. Had they done so, Count Alucard told himself, they would have gone directly to the stage-door, marched into his dressing-room and . . . The vegetarian vampire gulped and shivered as he considered the fate that might have overcome him. Then, recovering quickly, he reasoned that they would not recognise him now, just so long as they did not see his face.

Hearing Harcourt Hetherington clearing his throat in the wings, Count Alucard acted quickly. Rolling over on to his back on the still darkened stage, he hid his face from the audience. The two vampire hunters would not know him for who he was, if they only saw the back of his head.

The count had acted in the very nick of time.

He had barely managed to freeze his limbs into his "dead butler's body" position, when Harcourt Hetherington (in his Lord Maltravers' make-up and costume) strode onstage, flicking a switch by the door and flooding the Maltravers' drawing-room with light.

"Merciful heaven!" The old actor's voice boomed out over the stalls and carried up as far as the back row of the upper circle. "It is my dear old butler, Carstairs!" At which point, Mr Hetherington tossed back his silvery long hair and pointed a forefinger at the body on the carpet. "Dead! Dead!" he cried, then, "Who could have done this awful thing – and *why*? **WHY**?"

Harcourt Hetherington paused for dramatic effect, but the few moments of silence that followed were broken by a voice from the front stalls.

"You got it wrong, Sergeant!" Karl Gustaffe whispered loudly, unable to control his glee. "It isn't the butler that's the murderer, it's the butler that's been murdered. You've lost your bet – that's a grubeck you owe me!"

"A fat chance you've got of getting it," growled Alphonse Kropotel, annoyed both with himself at having wrongly guessed the murderer, and with his assistant for having raised the subject of the wager.

"*Ssshh!*" hissed an old lady fiercely. She was wearing a wide hat trimmed with artificial fruit and was sitting directly behind the vampire hunters. "Some of us are trying to watch the play!" she added, as she prodded the police sergeant firmly in his back with a podgy forefinger.

The two Tolokovonites held their silence from that moment on, and the play continued without further interruption. Some moments later, after several other actors had joined Lord Maltravers in the drawing-room, and while the plot was thickening nicely as they accused each other of being murderers, Count Alucard's nose began to itch.

At first, it seemed no more than a minor irritation – a ticklish sensation on the very tip of the vegetarian vampire's nose. Count Alucard, lying perfectly still on the drawing-room carpet, face hidden and back to the audience, felt sure that he would be able to put up with this small distraction. But as the minutes passed, and the occupants of Maltravers Hall argued all around him, the itching began to spread. All along one side of his nose and then down the other, and increasing in itchiness as it went, until it seemed as if there was an entire army of tiny creepy-crawlies running riot all over his face.

If only, Count Alucard agonised, he had been able to lift a hand and give his nose a good, long scratch! But that was the one thing that he daren't – *mustn't* – even think of doing. For one thing, he could not let his fellow actors down again – dead bodies did not scratch their noses. And, something else, he told himself: he should not forget the vampire hunters, sitting only metres away. If he were to move so much as a little finger, it would serve to draw attention to himself. No – no matter if his entire body were to itch all over, he could not take the risk and scratch himself.

Count Alucard lay motionless and suffered the itching torment which was now raging all across his face. He wondered how much more of the play there was to come. In an attempt to pass the time more quickly, he tried to banish the itching from his mind by concentrating his thoughts on other things. Pushing both the play and the vampire hunters to the back of his mind, the count turned his thoughts to his good friend, Henry Hollins. Count Alucard tried to picture his young friend at home in far-off Staplewood, and wondered what Henry might be doing at that very moment.

"But *why* can't we go to Transylvania, Dad?" asked Henry Hollins, puzzled. Believe it or not, but at the exact same moment that Count Alucard, stretched out on the theatre stage, was concentrating his thoughts on Henry Hollins, Henry Hollins's thoughts were fixed on his Transylvanian friend. "The count's invited us to go and stay with him at Alucard Castle," Henry continued, waving the count's letter in the air. "He'll be ever so disappointed if we don't turn up."

"I'm sorry, Henry," said Albert Hollins, sipping at his cup of cocoa. "But it's the busiest time of the year just now at the factory – I couldn't get away for a whole week if I wanted to." He paused, took a second sip at his cocoa, and then began again: "The thing is, Henry, your mum and I – "

"Don't put your cup down on that coffin without a coaster underneath it, Albert," broke in Emily Hollins. "I've spent most of this afternoon with a duster and a tin of furniture polish, putting a nice shine on that coffin-lid. Your cocoa-cup will leave a nasty ring."

"Sorry, Emily," said Mr Hollins hastily picking up his cup and transferring it on to the carpet between his feet before continuing to Henry, "As I was saying, Henry – your mum and I have been having a chat and this is what we have come up with, instead of doing the Transylvania thing. How about if we were to pop down to Wolverhampton this weekend, and spend a couple of nights with your Uncle Jim and Auntie Flo?"

"Oh," said Henry Hollins, glumly.

It wasn't that Henry didn't like his relations in the Midlands. On the contrary, Uncle Jim and Auntie Flo were as nice an uncle and aunt as any boy might wish for. But the prospect of a couple of evenings playing carpet bowls (Uncle Jim's obsession) in his relatives' sitting-room did not have quite the same appeal for Henry Hollins as that of a whole week of warm nights spent running wild in the Forest of Tolokovin, with the friendly wolf-pack howling around his heels and Count Alucard, in his fruit-bat form, flitting overhead.

"Cheer up, Henry," said Mrs Hollins, seeing the disappointment on her son's face. "There'll be lots of other times when we can go to Transylvania – and a weekend with Uncle Jim and Auntie Flo won't be all *that* bad . . ."

Unlike Henry, Emily Hollins was quite looking forward to the Wolverhampton weekend. For one thing, Emily was quite a dab hand at carpet bowls. Secondly, her sister, Flo, kept a home which was as neat and tidy as the proverbial new pin. And, while Emily had a soft spot in her heart for Henry's noble Transylvanian friend, she did have a few misgivings at the prospect of spending an entire week at Alucard Castle. There were the spiders' webs hanging at all the windows to be taken into consideration, while the dust on the ancient, carved long-table and the worn, leather-backed chairs in the stone-flagged dining hall looked as if it had been there as long as the furniture itself. Mrs Hollins gave a little shiver. She had never yet visited Alucard Castle without wishing that she had brought the box of polishes and dusters from the kitchen cupboard at 42, Nicholas Nickleby Close, Staplewood.

"I've got another little treat up my sleeve for you, Henry." Albert Hollins's voice broke in on Emily's thoughts as he addressed his son.

"What's that, Dad?"

"Well, I don't know whether you've had a chance to glance through this yet." As he spoke, Mr

Hollins picked up the copy of *The Garden Gnome Collector's Monthly* that had been resting on the coffin-lid, together with a couple of back issues of *The Coffin-Maker's Journal*, left behind by Count Alucard on a previous visit.

"Not yet, Dad." Henry Hollins shook his head. Although he tried his hardest to show an interest in his father's hobby and profession, Henry's pleasure at receiving the count's letter that day had driven all other matters from his mind.

"You're in for a surprise, then, when I tell you what's inside it," said Mr Hollins with a secretive chuckle, as he leafed through the pages of his magazine in search of the article in question. "Here we are!" Albert had found what he was looking for in the centre pages. But in order to keep the good news to himself for as long as possible, he hugged the open magazine to his chest. "This will please you too, Emily," he added, about to reveal his secret at last.

"Go on, Dad," said Henry, his interest finally aroused. "What is it?"

"Don't keep us all in suspense, Albert!" urged Emily.

"I suppose you had forgotten, both of you, that next week is National Garden Gnome Week?"

"I'd lose my head if it wasn't fastened on," said Emily Hollins, as an admission that the annual festivities in honour of the rosy-cheeked, white-bearded little people had slipped her mind. Henry, too, had been unaware that National Garden Gnome Week was about to pay its yearly visit. He nodded and hung his head in acknowledgement of his own forgetfulness.

"I don't know. You've got memories like sieves, the pair of you!" sighed Mr Hollins. "But now that I've reminded you, you won't need any further hints about which important event will be taking place at the weekend?"

"The Grand Garden Gnome Hunt," said Emily, without enthusiasm.

"Starting on Saturday morning," added Henry, "and finishing on Sunday night."

"The penny's dropped at last, and about time too!" cried Albert, turning round *The Garden Gnome Collector's Monthly* magazine and displaying the feature about the Garden Gnome Hunt which was spread across the centre pages.

The Grand Garden Gnome Hunt always marked the start of National Garden Gnome Week. Garden gnome lovers everywhere took to their cars, or bikes, or motorcycles – or even went on foot – and journeyed round town and countryside, peering into gardens, then writing down on entry forms the locations and descriptions of any garden gnomes that they might chance to spot. The Hunt was organised by *The Garden Gnome Collector's Monthly*, in conjunction with the Staplewood Garden Gnome Company Limited – the factory in which Albert Hollins worked. It was that firm which every year kindly donated the prizes to the three lucky entrants who had logged the most garden gnomes.

There was a rule on the official printed entry form which stated that neither the employees at the

Staplewood Garden Gnome factory nor immediate members of their families were allowed to enter the annual competition. But because of his keen interest and his love of garden gnomes, Albert Hollins took part every year, unofficially, without sending in an entry sheet. This was probably just as well, for if Mr Hollins had submitted the number of gnomes he sighted, he would have walked away with the first prize year after year.

"What I thought we might do this year," continued Albert across the coffin coffee-table, "is set off at the crack of dawn on Saturday morning and drive down to Uncle Jim's and Auntie Flo's in leisurely fashion – keeping off the motorway and going through the outskirts of a few small towns, then cruising through some out-of-the-way villages. That way we'll get to see the maximum of garden gnomes between here and Wolverhampton." Mr Hollins paused before adding eagerly, "What do you two think?"

Mrs Hollins exchanged a glance with Henry. They were both of the opinion that Wolverhampton was far enough away already without making the journey any longer. But neither of them wanted to seem a spoilsport by denying Albert his fun. After all, the Grand Garden Gnome Hunt *was* only once a year.

"That sounds a good idea, Albert," said Emily Hollins, faintly.

"Brilliant," said Henry Hollins, sounding glum.

"Then, on Sunday, we'll make another early day of it. We'll rope in Uncle Jim and Auntie Flo and cover every inch of Wolverhampton and its sur-

rounding area. It's all new territory down there for us."

"Whatever you say, Albert," sighed Emily. Henry, lost for words, could do no more than nod his head.

"I've been doing the groundwork already." As he spoke, Albert Hollins put out both of his hands and heaved at the coffin lid. The hinges, which needed oiling, let out a complaining squeal and the lid itself groaned as it moved upwards. Then, holding the coffin open, Albert slipped his free hand into the white satin-lined interior and lifted out a folded road map which had been resting on the lace-edged pillow. The coffin lid let out another moan as Mr Hollins lowered it gently back into place. "Now then," he continued, opening the road map and spreading it out across the coffin, "Here's what I've got planned . . ."

Henry and Emily Hollins stared at the road map, their spirits sinking. Albert had marked out his proposed route to Wolverhampton with a bright yellow, felt-tip marking-pen. The line looped, twisted, and double-backed on itself so many times that it might well have been made by a drunken snail meandering in the dark, without any idea where it was meant to be going.

"Golly," murmured Mrs Hollins.

"Gosh," muttered Henry. His shoulders drooped. He was not looking forward one little bit to the coming weekend. And his day had begun with such delight at receiving the letter from Count Alucard, coupled with his joy at the prospect of a trip to Transylvania. Suddenly, both Transylvania *and* Count Alucard seemed a very, *very* long way away.

8

"Hurrah! Bravo!"

The moment that the golden tassels stitched to the hem of the thick red curtain touched the stage, Karl Gustaffe was out of his seat, together with the rest of the audience, cheering and clapping noisily. Alphonse Kropotel was the only one to remain sitting – partly because he was afraid of dropping the black velvet bag containing the vampire destruction kit, and partly because he was a little cross with himself at not having guessed the murderer's identity.

The applause continued as the curtain rose again, to reveal the actors standing in a line at the front of the stage, holding hands and smiling out at the audience as they took their curtain calls. The company bowed three times in all. Then, because he was the most important member of the company, with twice as many words to learn as any of his fellow actors, Harcourt Hetherington stepped forward and gravely took a bow all by himself. The cheering rose to a crescendo as the old actor bowed so low from the waist that his long white hair almost touched the footlights.

"*Bravo*!" 'Well done!" The audience yelled, then

stamped its feet and whistled through its fingers. But on this occasion, Karl Gustaffe did not join in with the general applause. Something rather strange had occurred to the Tolokovin baker.

"That's odd!" murmured Gustaffe, as the curtain fell for the fourth and final time.

"What's odd?" muttered Kropotel, clambering to his feet at last, both arms clutching the precious bulky bag to his chest.

"Didn't you notice? When the actors took their bows, one of them wasn't there."

"Nonsense!" growled Kropotel. He did not like to think that a common fellow who pummelled dough for a living might have spotted something which a keen-eyed policeman, such as himself, could somehow have missed.

"It's true, Sergeant," the baker insisted. "The actor who played the dead body wasn't up there with the rest of them. I'm sure of it. I was particularly aware of his absence because I thought that he had played his part so well, I was going to give him an extra 'Bravo!' "

Police Sergeant Kropotel did not even bother to reply. The two vampire hunters were being swept along the auditorium's central aisle by the mass of exiting theatre-goers towards the foyer and the reality of the world outside. The evening's entertainment was over. Looking towards the exit doors, he could just glimpse the night sky. It was still raining – hard. The police sergeant had more important things to worry about than whether or not an actor had missed a curtain call.

"It's far too late to take up the hunt again

tonight," barked Alphonse Kropotel over his shoulder at his assistant. "We must seek out a place to lay our heads. Then we'll take up the search again at cock-crow, after a good night's sleep."

It was Karl Gustaffe's turn not to reply. After all, what was there to say? If the little baker could have had his way, he would have turned his nose Tolokovinwards there and then, and headed straight back towards his bakery. But he was not a baker any longer: he was his town's official assistant vampire hunter. Wherever the police sergeant chose to go, Karl Gustaffe had to follow. Alphonse Kropotel's word was law.

"Go to the cloakroom, Gustaffe, and get the luggage!" the chief vampire hunter barked at his assistant. "I'll meet you outside under the awning."

They had left the suitcase containing their clean clothing at the cloakroom when they had first arrived at the theatre. The bulky black velvet bag in Alphonse Kropotel's grasp was far too important to be entrusted to a cloakroom attendant.

Karl Gustaffe sighed and felt in his pocket for the half-grubeck cloakroom fee as he moved to obey. By rights, the cloakroom money should have come out of the bag of coins which Mayor Rumboll had given to the policeman to cover the expenses of the vampire hunt. But the little baker knew that there was small chance of Alphonse Kropotel coughing up half a grubek if he could possibly help it! The sergeant *was* wrong about that actor too, Gustaffe told himself. "He *wasn't* up on that stage with the others at the end of the play. I wondered where he'd got to?"

The assistant vampire hunter had not been alone in noticing the butler's absence at the curtain call. Harcourt Hetherington had also realised that one of his cast was missing from the line-up.

Standing on the stage, holding hands with the cast members standing on either side of him while waiting for the curtain to rise in order that they might take their bows, the old actor had glanced along the line in both directions at his assembled company. Harcourt Hetherington always made this last-minute check, to ensure that his actors were properly assembled and correctly dressed. Horror of horrors, some years before, one inexperienced young actor had had a quick costume change to make in the last scene of a play, and had taken the curtain call with his trousers unzipped and his underpants gaping through, plain for all the audience to see! Tonight Mr Hetherington had been dismayed to discover that, himself included, there were eight cast members standing in the line, instead of the required nine! It had not taken him very long to realise which one of his actors had gone absent without seeking his permission.

"Where's Mr Alucard?" the white-haired actor had hissed across at Grantley Hardcastle, who was standing in the wings, waiting for the signal to raise the curtain.

In answer, Hardcastle had given a bewildered shrug of his shoulders and said, "I don't know, Mr Hetherington – shall I hold the curtain and send somebody to look for him?"

"Certainly not!" Harcourt Hetherington nodded in the direction of the audience, invisible beyond the curtain, but making their presence known as they applauded what had gone before. "The public are eager to offer us their appreciation – we must take our curtain calls tonight without benefit of Mr Alucard. But I shall have some strong words to say to that gentleman when I do see him, believe me, Mr Hardcastle! Take up the curtain!"

Grantley Hardcastle took a firm grip on the iron wheel and, as he swung it round, the curtain began to rise as the audience's applause grew in volume. Harcourt Hetherington, experienced actor that he was, had changed the frown on his face for a wistful smile before the curtain had risen beyond his chin. He tightened his grip on the hands of the actors standing on his either side.

Harcourt Hetherington had been an actor all of his adult life, but he still felt a thrill surge through his entire body every time he stood in the glow of the footlights at the end of a play, and drank in the audience's applause. On this particular night, in the final moments before he led his colleagues in the first of their bows, he was pleased to see that the entire audience was up on its feet and awarding his company with a standing ovation – with the exception, that is, of one fellow with a pointed moustache in the second row of the stalls, who had remained sitting, clutching a bulky black velvet bag.

Sitting in his dressing-room, gazing despondently into the empty mirror, Count Alucard blinked nervously as he heard the sharp knock on the door.

"Mr Alucard?" Harcourt Hetherington sounded very angry. "Are you in there?"

For almost a second, but not longer, the vegetarian vampire wondered whether to lie low and pretend that he was somewhere else. But what would have been the good of that? he asked himself. He would have to face up to his employer's anger, sooner or later.

"Come in, Mr Hetherington!" the count called back, but not before he had had the good sense to slide off his chair, for obvious reasons, and back on to the dressing-room floor.

"Surely you're not *still* looking for that dressing-room key?" snapped Harcourt Hetherington, even more annoyed at finding the actor on his hands and knees for a second time. "I suppose it was the missing key that made you forget to appear for the curtain call?"

"I'm afraid it was," replied Count Alucard, snatching gratefully at the excuse that had been provided for him. In fact, the vegetarian vampire had absented himself from the curtain call because he had known that there were two vampire hunters sitting in the audience. The moment that the curtain had been brought down on the play's last scene, and temporary darkness had followed, Count Alucard had leapt to his feet from his "dead body" position, and scuttled off to the dressing-room as fast as his long, spindly legs would carry him. For he knew full well that to have presented himself, face-front and standing upright in the curtain call line-up, would have been just about the most foolish thing that he could possibly have done. "I am most *awfully* sorry," he continued to his employer. "And I do assure you, with all of my heart, that it won't ever happen again."

"If only it were just your absence at the final curtain, Mr Alucard, I might have been able to find it in my heart to overlook your abominable behaviour . . ." The old actor paused, his temper rising, and he brushed his fingers angrily through a lock of long, white hair which had fallen over his forehead. "But there was also the disgraceful business of you forgetting your speech at the beginning of the play."

"What can I say, sir, except to repeat that I am deeply, *deeply* sorry!" murmured the vegetarian vampire, blinking up at his employer from the floor.

"*Sorry?*" Harcourt Hetherington's cheeks puffed out as his face turned red and, for a moment, it seemed as if he were about to burst. "Good heavens above, my fine fellow! You only had four words to learn – " The old actor paused again, and suddenly felt uncomfortable as he found his gaze drawn towards the vampire's pale, forlorn face. Count Alucard's red-rimmed eyes appeared to be brimming with tears. Despite his anger, Harcourt

Hetherington could not help but feel a sudden surge of sympathy for the odd individual staring up at him. Good gracious me! the old actor told himself. I do believe the chap's about to weep! But, aloud, he said, "There, there! Come, come, old fellow – things can't be that bad!"

"But they are!" The vegetarian vampire gulped, and now a single tear welled in the corner of one eye. The Transylvanian nobleman, almost overcome with self-pity, managed to blink back the tear. "I've let you down – and I've let my fellow actors down." His shoulders trembled as he let out a little sob.

"I'm sure they'll manage to forgive you for it," said Harcourt Hetherington who, despite his stern appearance, was really a kind person at heart. "After all," he continued encouragingly, "there were some *good* things about your performance tonight."

"Were there?" asked Count Alucard, eagerly.

"Oh yes, indeed! Frankly speaking, I thought that your portrayal of the dead body was absolutely superb!"

"Did you *really*?" Count Alucard's mood had swung from deepest gloom to purest joy – and in a trice. He preened himself as, seeking further compliments, he added, "You're not just saying that?"

"Not at all. I thought that, as the dead butler, you gave the performance of a lifetime."

"It's extremely kind of you to say so," said Count Alucard. He had suddenly arrived at the opinion that a career in the theatre might not be such a bad thing after all.

"And now, if you'll excuse me, I must get out of costume myself," said the old actor. "I have to see that all the props and scenery are safely stowed inside the van. You must either find that dressing-room key rather smartly, or else forget all about it. We're setting off for our next venue tonight, you know. We assemble outside the theatre, where the coach will be waiting, at eleven o'clock prompt." Then, stepping over Count Alucard's outstretched, spindly legs, Harcourt Hetherington opened the door.

"I'll be there," the count called up at the old actor, adding, "By the way, where exactly is the next theatre at which we are booked to appear?"

But Harcourt Hetherington had already gone.

I cannot imagine what came over me, murmured the bewildered Harcourt Hetherington, to himself, outside the vampire's dressing-room. "I went in there intending to give that chap a ticking off – I seem to have ended up showering him with praise!"

But Count Alucard often had that effect on strangers. Those who were not aware of his vampirical connections were quick to warm to the count's odd, friendly personality. Folk who did know about his family history were more likely to keep their distance.

"Is this the best you've got to offer?" asked

Sergeant Kropotel, grumpily. He was standing with Karl Gustaffe in the open doorway of a dirty attic room, with peeling wallpapered walls and floorboards carpeted with dust.

"It's *all* I've got to offer," replied Gunter Hasselflugel, the shabbily dressed owner of the lodging-house which was situated on the outskirts of the city. "Take it or leave it."

"How much?" asked the police sergeant.

"Five grubecks." As he spoke, Hasselflugel scratched at his chin in pursuit of a flea which had taken up lodgings in his thick, black beard some days before.

"*Five*?" It was the little baker who had echoed the words in some dismay. Five grubecks was about as much as he earned, back home in Tolokovin, after slaving over a hot oven all day.

"It's up to you," said the lodging-house keeper, with a shrug and a shiver. There was a chill wind blowing through a crack in the attic-landing windowframe. "I can't stand here all night arguing with you two."

The vampire hunters allowed their eyes to roam around the uninviting room. Apart from two iron bedsteads, each of which possessed a filthy mattress and a threadbare blanket, there was not much in the way of furniture. There was an empty packing-case against one wall, which did duty as a bedside table, and a greasy empty oil-lamp drum across the room, which served a similar duty. The attic did not boast a wardrobe, but there were a couple of big, rusting nails sticking out behind the door as coat-hooks. The only decorative item was an

unframed Saint Unfortunato poster on the wall (the martyr pictured, as always, with the blood spurting out from the holes where his arms and legs had been, before his enemies chopped them off). Originally there had been four drawing-pins holding up the poster, but one of these had been borrowed by a previous lodger and now a top corner was hanging down, hiding the martyr's face. The only other object in the attic was a large wooden bucket in the centre of the floor.

Spotting the bucket simultaneously and guessing at its purpose, both Kropotel and Gustaffe turned their eyes towards the raftered ceiling. They had guessed correctly. The bucket was there to catch any rain that might fall in through the hole in the roof.

"The roof leaks." It was the chief vampire hunter who made this observation.

"That hole serves two purposes," replied Gunter Hasselfugel, holding up the lantern he was carrying so that the two men might better see the aperture. "It may or may not have come to your attention, gentlemen, but this room does not possess a window. Luckily, you'll know that morning has come when sunlight shines through the roof. Also, if it should chance to rain again during the night, you'll have fresh water in the morning for a wash."

"Do you provide soap and a towel?" asked the baker, hopefully.

"Soap and a towel? You'll be lucky! Where do you think you are? The Transylvanian Hilton Hotel?" The lodging-house keeper struck the palm of his hand smartly across his cheek, in an attempt to kill off the tiny lodger in his beard, but without success. "Look – do you want the place, or don't you? Yes or no?"

The vampire hunters exchanged a glance. They had walked for miles through driving rain which had accompanied them most of the way. Karl Gustaffe had lugged the suitcase; Alphonse Kropotel had hugged the vampire destruction kit in its black velvet bag close to his chest. They were cold, wet and tired. Suddenly the iron bedsteads, the filthy mattresses and the threadbare blankets seemed rare luxuries.

"We'll take it," said the sergeant of police.

"Money in advance," replied Gunter Hasselflugel, thrusting out an eager, dirty, open hand.

"When are you going to blow that candle out, Gustaffe, and go to sleep?" grumbled Alphonse Kropotel, pulling the thin blanket up around his ears and peering across the attic at where his companion was sitting up in the other bed.

"Sorry, Sergeant," said the little baker, hugging his knees which were tucked up underneath his chin.

The same wind that rattled the windowframe out on the landing whistled in under the attic door, making the flame of the candle on Karl Gustaffe's oil-drum bedside table dance; it cast strange, moving shadows across the raftered ceiling. The moving shadows and the whistling wind had combined to put the midnight dread of vampires into Karl Gustaffe's head, so that it was impossible for him to sleep. But the baker knew full well that, were he to extinguish the candle-flame, the dark of night in these unfamiliar surroundings would bring more terrors than the flickering light. But how could a vampire hunter own up to his superior officer that he was afraid of the dark?

"I think that all today's adventures must have made me *over*-tired," Karl Gustaffe lied. "I'll let the candle burn just a few minutes longer, and have a read in bed – that's what I usually do when I'm back home in Tolokovin, if I can't get off to sleep."

"You're not in Tolokovin," growled Sergeant Kropotel. "You're here. In this empty attic. There isn't anything to read. Blow out the candle – and be quick about it!"

Karl Gustaffe's eyes darted, urgently, all around the dingy room.

Alphonse Kropotel had spoken the truth. There was not a book or magazine or newspaper, or any other kind of reading matter, in that sparsely furnished room. Karl Gustaffe gulped. The very idea of total darkness made his heart race, pit-a-pat! Spurred on by fear, he suddenly had a brilliant thought.

"I know what I can read, Sergeant!" Sliding his feet from underneath the threadbare blanket, Karl Gustaffe lowered them to the floor. Then, after crossing the room on tiptoe (in order not to cover the soles of his feet with dust), he felt inside the pockets of his jacket which was hanging next to Sergeant Kropotel's uniform on one of the nails behind the door.

Karl Gustaffe heaved a sigh of relief. It was still there. Thank goodness! "Here's a stroke of luck, Sergeant!" he said, holding up the theatre programme he had bought earlier that evening. "It's a good job I didn't throw this away."

But as he tiptoed back towards the iron bed, attempting to place his toes in the dust-free toeprints he had made on his outward crossing, a slip of printed paper slid out from between the programme's pages and wafted on to the floorboards.

"What's that?" asked Alphonse Kropotel.

"Don't know, Sergeant." The little baker stooped, retrieved the slip of paper, then took it over to his bed and held it up to the flickering flame of the candle on the oil-drum beside table.

"By the holy beard of Saint Unfortunato," gasped Karl Gustaffe. "Come and look at this, Sergeant!"

Without a word, Alphonse Kropotel threw off his blanket and raced across the room, not caring if he should get his feet covered in dust. Together, the two vampire hunters studied the printed message on the slip of paper.

IMPORTANT NOTICE
Cast Alteration
At tonight's performance, the part of
CARSTAIRS, THE BUTLER
will be portrayed by
MR C. ALUCARD, Esq.

"What do you think, Sergeant?" murmured Gustaffe. "Is it possible that this Mr C. Alucard Esq. is really . . .?"

"Of course he is!" snapped the policeman. "There's only one man on this earth called Alucard so far as I am aware. I say 'man', but I mean 'vile monster'. And, now I come to cast my mind back, I thought there was something familiar about that dead body's back, during the whole time that it was lying there on stage, in front of our very eyes!" But Sergeant Kropotel did not have time to waste on conversation. He raced across the attic, grabbed his uniform from the nail behind the door, then hopped, first on one foot, then on the other, as he tried to put his feet into his socks in double-quick time. In doing so, the chief vampire hunter lost his balance and fell over on to the floor.

"More haste, less speed, Sergeant," observed his assistant.

"Don't just stand there watching." growled the policeman as he picked himself up. "Get dressed!"

"Dressed, Sergeant? Me, Sergeant? *Now*?"

"Yes! Yes! Yes!" barked Kropotel, in answer to all three of his subordinate's questions.

"Why? Where are we going?"

"Vampire hunting, you fool. Where else?" Alphonse Kropotel's medals jangled against each other as he snatched up his jacket. His boots, he noticed, were badly in need of a polish – but there was no time for that.

"At this hour of the night?" asked Karl Gustaffe, bleakly.

"Of course. We are officially appointed vampire hunters. It is our bounden duty to take action at every sighting of the monster. Get into your clothes."

The baker moved to obey, but without enthusiasm. He paused again, and his face fell even further as he pointed upwards. "Look, Sergeant Kropotel!" he wailed. "Look up there!"

The two Tolokovonites had taken some small comfort, as they lay shivering in their beds, in the fact that the rain, at least, had stopped. But now, even Alphonse Kropotel's appetite for the chase was momentarily dulled as his eyes turned upwards and followed his assistant's outstretched, shaking forefinger.

Up in the rafters, in the flickering shadows caused by the candle's light, a couple of large snow-flakes were plainly visible, drifting down towards the floorboards. As Kropotel and Gustaffe stared up at the hole in the ceiling, the first pair of snowflakes were quickly followed by a threesome, and then a whole flurry entered close on the heels of those that had gone before.

"It's snowing, Sergeant."

"I can see that it's snowing," growled the sergeant of police. "But I never heard of a vampire hunt being called off for the sake of a few snowflakes." The police sergeant paused long enough to tug the black velvet bulky bag from under his bed, where he had hidden it for safety's sake, then strode across and opened the door. "For the last time, you wretched shrubel-cake maker, get into your clothes and follow me – or I shall come back and drag you outside in your underclothes!" With which words, Sergeant Kropotel turned and hurried off, his heavy boots clattering on the rickety stairs.

But it was not Alphonse Kropotel's threat that caused the little baker to dress more quickly now than he had ever done before – it was the fear of being left all alone in the top-floor room, with the wind whistling on the landing, and the shadows dancing among the rafters.

Karl Gustaffe was into his things and racing down the top flight of stairs before his fellow vampire hunter had reached the bottom of the lowest flight, in the lodging-house's shabby hall.

9

Albert Ridley, the driver of the coach, tugged nervously at the brim of his cloth cap, then rubbed hard at the windscreen with his coat-sleeve. Leaning forward, he breathed on the glass, then rubbed with his sleeve again, even harder. But without success. "It's not a bit of good," he announced over his shoulder to his anxious passengers. "We can't go any further tonight – we'll just have to stop where we are."

"But my dear good fellow, we *must* go on!" declared Harcourt Hetherington, rising in his seat. "We have simply got to reach the Transylvanian border before tomorrow morning. We have a very tight schedule to which we must adhere at all costs!"

The Transylvanian border? Count Alucard, sitting alone on the back seat of the coach, digested this information and allowed himself a little smile. In the haste of helping his fellow actors and the stagehands take down the scenery, pack the costumes and props in theatrical hampers, and load all of these into the back of the big van, he had quite forgotten to enquire where the next performance of the play was going to take place. But the very fact that they were going anywhere at all was good news as far as the count was concerned. Every mile they journeyed along the road was one mile further from the vampire hunters who were trying to track him down. Except that at the moment both the coach and the van, which had braked behind it, weren't travelling anywhere at all. They had come to a standstill.

"You show me where the road is, Mr Hetherington, and I'll be only too delighted to drive along it," said Albert Ridley, in reply to the old actor's command. Then, nodding out through the windscreen, the coach driver continued, "But just you take a look out there and then see if you can tell me which way I'm supposed to go, because I'm flummoxed if I know!"

All along the coach, the passengers pressed their noses to the windows and peered out into the moonlit night. Albert Ridley was telling the truth – the road ahead had vanished completely, hidden beneath a carpet of snow which stretched away as far as the eye could see.

The coach, and the scenery van behind it, had pulled up in a clearing on the fringes of a Transylvanian forest. The snowstorm had been brief but heavy. Moments before, they had been travelling along a bumpy, narrow road which wound between tall fir trees with a wealth of spring flowers spread out on either side. But springtime showers in that part of the world can all too quickly turn to wintry snow. Although the snow was not too thick for the coach's wheels to pass through, it was deep enough to have covered the road completely. What's more, at that late hour and in that lonely part of Transylvania, without a sign of human life in any direction, it was unlikely that they would meet up with any other transport.

"Are you saying, Albert, that we're going to have to spend the night here?" asked Grantley Hardcastle, who was sitting in the front seat next to the driver.

"It certainly begins to look that way, Grantley," replied Albert Ridley, adding, "Unless you've got any other suggestions?"

"Then we shall just have to make the best of it, I suppose," said the stage-manager, pulling his coat collar up around his ears.

"Oh heavens!" called out one of the actors. "We shall surely freeze to death out here in this wilderness!" The young actor's name was Ashley Stevenson. He had the small role of a constable in *Murder At Maltravers Hall* and he also understudied the part of Sir Archie Granville. Ashley Stevenson was a nice enough chap, but a little on the excitable side. "They'll discover our frozen corpses in the morning!" he added.

An anxious murmur rippled all along the coach. Several passengers fidgeted in their seats. Actors, generally, are nervous folk by nature and Ashley Stevenson's fears were catching. Then something else happened to put them even more on edge – the stillness of the moonlit night was broken sharply by an animal cry that rose and fell from somewhere deep in the forest.

"*Ah-whooo-OOOOO-ooooooh*!"

"Wolves!" The cry came from a small, plump

lady with dark frizzy hair, gold-rimmed spectacles perched on the end of her nose, and several strings of long, black beads which dangled over a lace-edged white blouse. Her name was Millie Pilkington and she was the company's wardrobe mistress. "We'll all be eaten alive!" she wailed.

"*Ah-whooo-OOOOOOOH*!" The first wolf-call was answered by another.

Most of the passengers, by now, were leaping to their feet. Ashley Stevenson was wondering whether, for safety's sake, he might clamber up and hide himself on the luggage-rack. The young actress, Lucy Lanebury, had moved out into the aisle and was whimpering as she nibbled nervously at the hem of her handkerchief. Pandemonium was but seconds away.

"Ladies! Gentlemen! Pray calm yourselves, I do beseech you! Believe me, there is absolutely no cause for panic whatsoever!" It was Count Alucard's firm voice that brought the passengers to their senses. As one, they turned and looked at the tall, thin, pale-faced, black-suited figure addressing them from the back of the bus. The count waited until he had their full attention. He had thought of a plan by which he might not only calm their fears, but also solve the problem of the road ahead which now lay hidden by the snow. "There may well be a pack of wolves roaming the forest," he finally continued, "but those animals do not mean you any harm, of that I can assure you."

The passengers exchanged curious glances, wondering whether they could trust the word of this recent recruit to their theatrical band. How could a man who had acted the part of a dead butler earlier that evening, they asked themselves, also be an expert in the behaviour of wolves?

"And how can you be sure of what you say, Mr Alucard?" It was the company's leading actor himself who voiced the question that all of them were thinking. Harcourt Hetherington had remained reasonably calm while all the rest had been close to panic, and he was eager now to hear what his apprentice actor had to say. He was beginning to suspect that there was more to Mr C. Alucard, Esq. than met the eye . . . "Come, come, sir! Explain yourself."

"Well . . ." The Transylvanian nobleman paused before replying. He knew that he would need to choose his words very carefully indeed. If his plan was going to succeed, he would have to explain it to the passengers without giving away the fact that it was vampire blood that coursed through his veins. That information *would* cause panic! In short, he told himself, it would be necessary for him to lie to the coach passengers, but only for their own good. "I was born and bred in this part of the world," he said at last. "And I know enough about this region to know the wolves that dwell here are sadly misunderstood – they have never attacked a human being in all of their lives – well, not without good reason." So far, he had told nothing less than the truth. Then, hearing the murmurs of disbelief and seeing again the exchange of doubtful glances, he continued quickly, "My dear late father was an authority on wildlife conservation. He was responsible for the wellbeing of all the forest wolves.

Because of his work, he knew every single wolf that roamed hereabouts. And, when I was a child, he introduced me to them." Then, as the disbelieving murmurs grew in volume, and the doubtful glances increased in number, the count strode down the coach, elbowing his way past his fellow actors, as he added, "And I shall prove it to you!"

At which point, having arrived at the front of the coach, the count leaned forward and, accompanied by a concerted gasp of horror from all of those on board, he tugged open the door.

"Don't go out there, Mr Alucard!" murmured Miss Pilkington, her fingers clutching at her beads. "You are sure to be torn to pieces!"

"Close that door at once!" begged Ashley Stevenson. "Or we shall *all* be torn to pieces!"

"Believe me, there is nothing to be feared," said the count with a chuckle. "Although, until my friends, the children of the night, are better accustomed to your presence, it might be best if you were to shut this door behind me."

With that, Count Alucard leaped off the coach and landed lightly in his black, shiny shoes on the snow below. Mindful of the warning, Albert Ridley leaned across and closed the door; then, just to be on the safe side, he pressed the switch that locked it tight. The members of the Hetherington Players crowded at the windows along one side of the coach, and peered out at the count as he crossed into the centre of the snow-covered clearing.

"*Ah-whoooo-OOOOOH*!" Count Alucard threw back his head and imitated perfectly the call of a wolf. "*Ah-whoooo-OOOOOOH*" he went again.

Then, as the row of faces gathered at the windows watched in growing astonishment, in ones and twos, then threes and fours, a score of wolves and more padded out of the pine trees and crossed over to Count Alucard. They nuzzled against his legs and vied with each other as they tried to push their noses into his outstretched hand.

"He was telling us the truth," murmured Grantley Hardcastle, scarcely able to believe what he was looking at. "He *is* their friend. They *like* him!"

"The more I see of Mr Alucard, the more he continues to surprise me," observed Harcourt Hetherington, half to himself. "But this much I will say," added the old actor, as he watched the wolves almost knock over the vegetarian vampire in their eagerness to get close to him, "there is something about that chappie that intrigues me."

"Hello, Misha! Good girl, Olga! Easy, Drushka! Steady, Franz, you'll knock me over!" Count Alucard greeted each wolf in turn by name, affording every single one either a friendly pat under the jowls or a gentle slap across the haunches. No matter how far the vegetarian vampire travelled across Transylvania, as long as he stayed close to thc wide-ranging forests, the wolves were never very far away.

When greetings had been exchanged between the animals and the vampire, the count bent down and whispered a few words to Boris, the wise leader of the wolf-pack. The old silver-grey wolf pricked up his ears and panted eagerly, tongue lolling, to show that he had understood. A moment later, the leader had turned and bounded off across the snowy wasteland, with the rest of the pack in close pursuit.

Count Alucard waited until his friends were lost from sight and then he turned and crunched back across the snow towards the coach. As the black-clad figure approached, and knowing that the wolves had gone, Albert Ridley leaned across again to unlock and open the door.

"Switch on your headlights," the count commanded as he leaped on board.

The coach driver obeyed. Across the snow, in the sharp, clear beam of light, a straight line of close-trodden wolves' tracks were plainly visible, stretching off through the fringe of pine trees and beyond, as far as the eye could see.

"Follow that trail," said the count.

"But those are wild animals' tracks," objected Albert Ridley, taking off his check cloth cap with one hand and scratching at his balding head with the other. "How can we be sure that they will lead us where we want to go?"

"Do as Mr Alucard says, Albert," ordered Harcourt Hetherington. Then, as the coach driver revved up his engine, the old actor patted the empty seat beside him. "In my humble opinion, my dear fellow," he said, smiling up at the count encouragingly, "it is high time that you and I exchanged a few serious words."

"I think that you are most probably right," said the count with a sigh, for he was not the kind of person who liked facing up to situations. "Where would you like me to start?" he asked after he had sat down, gazing into his employer's face out of red-rimmed, dark, anxious eyes.

"Why not try the beginning?" said Harcourt Hetherington. "I have always found that to be the most appropriate starting place."

Count Alucard hesitated. But only for a second. He knew that he would have to unburden himself to someone – and something told him that the white-haired old actor was a man who could be trusted. "It all began with my great-great-great-grandfather," said Count Alucard, after having taken a deep breath. "His name was Count Dracula – "

"Great heavens!" gulped Harcourt Hetherington. "I do apologise for interrupting. Do go on . . ."

Slowly at first, and with the sharp beam from the headlights picking up the wolves' tracks, the coach bumped along the snow-covered road. Close in its tyre-tracks, also with headlamps ablaze, came the lorry which contained the theatrical company's scenery and props. Under the Transylvanian moon, hanging low in the starry sky, the two vehicles moved off over the snow-covered countryside.

Alphonse Kropotel and Karl Gustaffe arrived at last outside the entrance to the theatre. It had not been an easy task for them to retrace their steps through the maze of streets, from the lodging-house on the outskirts, back to the theatre in the centre of the city. It was late at night. The streets were deserted, so they could not ask their way. The street-lamps were switched off and the shop windows were dark. Coupled with all of which, and worst of all, there had been the falling snow to further hinder the two men's progress.

There's one good thing to be said for it, Karl Gustaffe had told himself as they set out from the lodging-house, "at least I'm not required to lug that big heavy suitcase everywhere we go."

It had been Sergeant Kropotel's decision to leave their baggage behind in the attic room, in order not to slow them down. They could go back for it later, the policeman reasoned, after they had caught up with and destroyed the vampire. But the fact that the suitcase had been left behind did not mean that the little baker went empty-handed.

"You can take your turn at carrying this instead,"

Alphonse Kropotel had snapped, thrusting the bulky black velvet bag into the assistant vampire hunter's arms, the moment they had stepped into the street.

"Thanks very much," the baker had said, sarcastically.

And thus they had arrived, about an hour later, outside the theatre – only to find that they were too late. The Hetherington Players had moved on. Even the poster announcing *Murder At Maltravars Hall* had gone – or was being replaced as they arrived. A thickset man with a straggly beard, wearing two thick overcoats as protection against the weather, was perched up on a ladder, pasting a new poster over the previous one on the theatre's billboard:

Commencing Monday
For One Week Only
GRUNWALD'S FAMOUS PUPPETS
Fun For All The Family
Admission: One grubek
Children: Half-price

"Hullo there!" called the bill-sticker, glancing down at the two vampire hunters standing close by the foot of his ladder. His name was Helmut Zimmerman and, in his lonely late-night profession, he seldom got the chance to talk to people. "Where are you two bound for at this time of night?"

"Don't let him know the nature of our business,"

hissed Alphonse Kropotel at his assistant. "A man who works all through the hours of darkness could easily be in league with vampires. But engage the fellow in conversation, Gustaffe, and see what you can find out from him without giving anything away."

"Find out about what, Sergeant?"

"About the vampire we're looking for, you fool!"

"Hullo yourself!" called out the baker, turning his gaze towards the man up the ladder. Several moments then went by while Karl Gustaffe racked his brains as to how he might prolong the conversation without 'giving anything away'. "Will you tell me something?" he said at last.

"If I know the answer to the question," replied the two-overcoated bill-poster obligingly.

"It's about the Grunwald Puppets," said Gustaffe, nodding up at the poster which Zimmerman was sticking to the billboard.

"What about them?"

"Are they glove-puppets or are they string-puppets – *Ouch*!" The final "*Ouch*!" had not been intended for the bill-poster's ears, but was grunted by Karl Gustaffe after receiving Alphonse Kropotel's elbow, sharply, in his ribs. "That hurt!" he whispered.

"It was meant to hurt, you idiot!" the policeman hissed back. "Why are you cross-questioning him about the puppets? Where do you imagine that line of enquiry will get you?"

"You told me not to arouse his suspicions, Sergeant," the little baker murmured back, then added, "Besides, I *would* like to learn something about the puppets. I like puppets."

"That's a difficult one to answer," said Helmut Zimmerman. He had been turning Karl Gustaffe's question over in his head and had not heard the urgent whispered conversation between the vampire hunters. "Some of them are glove puppets and some of them are string puppets," he went on, dipping his brush into the pot of paste that was hanging from a rung of his ladder and slapping it energetically across the billboard. "While several of them are so large that it takes three of the puppeteers to control each one, with long sticks."

"Goodness gracious!" gasped Karl Gustaffe, then, "*Ouch!*" he grunted for a second time, as Alphonse Kropotel's elbow struck him, even harder, in the same spot as before.

"I beg your pardon?" said the bill-poster.

"Never mind the puppets!" It was Sergeant Kropotel's turn to take up the conversation. "What do you know about the actors who were in the play which was advertised on the poster underneath the one you are sticking up?"

"Not much," said Helmut Zimmerman with a shrug. "What was it you wished to know?"

"Which town they have gone on to from here? Where will they be appearing next?"

"Nowhere," replied the bill-poster. As he spoke, he slapped on the last piece of the Grunwald's Puppets poster, completely covering up the one advertising *Murder At Maltravers Hall*.

"Nowhere?" wailed Alphonse Kropotel, and his voice rang out in the darkness of the night. "They can't have gone nowhere! There's no such place as nowhere!"

"That's true enough," replied Helmut Zimmerman as he made his way down the ladder, carefully carrying the pot of paste. "But they're certainly not appearing anywhere in Transylvania – and that's a fact."

"Perhaps they've gone back to England, Sergeant?" suggested Karl Gustaffe. "They were English actors."

The moment that the words had left his mouth, the little baker could have kicked himself for having spoken them aloud. Perhaps he had misguidedly hoped that by suggesting their quarry had left the country, he might prompt the police sergeant into calling off the vampire hunt. But Karl Gustaffe should have known by now that his superior officer was not that kind of man. Once Sergeant Kropotel got his teeth into anything, he did not let go easily. That was how he had worked his way up through the ranks, from police constable to police sergeant. That was why he had been appointed to lead the vampire hunt. That was why there would be no turning back.

"By heavens, Gustaffe, I think you've got it!" roared Alphonse Kropotel, so excited that he failed to reprimand his assistant for calling him "Sergeant" in front of the bill-posting suspect. "Come on!" he added, seizing the baker's hand and half-dragging him along the snow-covered pavement.

"Where are we going to, Sergeant?"

"Why, to England of course, you dolt! Where else!"

Crazy! They are both crazy! murmured Helmut Zimmerman to himself as he watched the two Tolokovonites set off back the way they had come, retracing their footsteps in the snow. "You would do better to stay in Transylvania!" he yelled after them. "If it is entertainment that you seek, then the Grunwald Puppets are ten times better than the English actors, any day of the week!"

But Helmut Zimmerman's advice came too late. Alphonse Kropotel and Karl Gustaffe were already out of earshot. The Transylvanian bill-poster sighed and shook his head as the two vampire hunters vanished from sight. Then, setting down the paste-pot and brush, he tugged both of his overcoat collars up around his ears and settled the canvas bag containing the Grunwald Puppet posters more comfortably across his shoulders, before retrieving the brush and paste-pot. After spitting into the snow, Helmut Zimmerman trudged off into the night, in the direction of his next billboard.

Albert Ridley began to whistle softly, so as not to disturb the passengers, and drummed his fingers on the steering-wheel in time to his tune. Although he had been driving now for several hours without a break, he had good reason to be cheerful. It was that last hour of dark before the coming of dawn. The road ahead was clear. The snow had disappeared many miles behind and the wolves had veered away an hour or so before, their task completed, and headed back towards the shelter of the forest. The coach wheels were travelling smoothly along the even, country road. Before very long, they would reach the turn off on to the Transylvanian motorway.

"From which point on, Albert, my old chum," the coach driver chuckled to himself, "it will be easy-peasy, all systems go and Bob's your uncle, all the way to the Channel Ferry . . ."

The coach driver glanced back over his left shoulder. The reading lights above the seats along the coach were dimmed. The actors, the stage-crew and the other company members were sprawled out, eyes closed and fast asleep. Miss Pilkington, the wardrobe mistress, stirred in her slumbers and then settled again. Grantley Hardcastle, his mouth open, was snoring gently:

"Awwwww-ZZZZZ-zzzzzz. . . AwwwwwZZZZ-Zzzzzz . . ."

Two of the passengers were not asleep. Despite the fact that the coach was in darkness, Harcourt Hetherington and Count Alucard had stayed wide awake all through the night. It was the Transylvanian nobleman who had been doing all the talking, while the actor had listened to the vegetarian vampire's tale with growing wonder. Count Alucard did not often unburden his history to anyone, but when he finally resolved on such a plan, he did not hold back any secrets.

"And so what you are telling me, Mr Alucard," broke in Harcourt Hetherington, his voice kept low, his bushy eyebrows rising in disbelief, "is that you are a real, live Transylvanian vampire!"

"I'm afraid so," replied the count, running his tongue nervously around his lips and over his two pointy teeth. He was still not sure how his employer would react to this information. "An accident of birth, sad to say – all of my ancestors were similarly creatures of the night."

"And, like all vampires, you have the amazing ability to turn yourself into a bat?"

"Indeed I do possess that talent. But only during the hours of darkness, naturally. Except that, unlike other vampires, I become a fruit-bat. Believe me, I have no taste whatsoever for human blood." The count pulled a face and gave a delicate shiver of distaste at the very idea of such a practice. "A ripe purple plum or a juicy fleshy peach are all that I have ever hungered after in my whole life.

"And yet you say that, even as we speak, there are vampire hunters out to take your life?"

"It's true!" Count Alucard wailed. He raised his hands in horror and his long, pale fingers fluttered as he contemplated his impending doom. "They want to drive a wooden stake into my heart! Can you believe it? That's why I sought refuge in the theatre last night."

"It is the most extraordinary story that I have ever heard in all my born days," said Harcourt Hetherington, staring long and hard into Count Alucard's red-rimmed eyes. "And I would very much like to believe you – "

"Are you accusing me of telling fibs?" the count broke in.

"Well . . ." The old actor paused, shrugged his shoulders and ran his fingers, thoughtfully through his long white hair, before continuing, "I do have to say, sir, that your narrative does seem a little far-fetched."

"Far-fetched!" wailed the count indignantly. "But you saw for yourself, Mr Hetherington, the friendship that exists between myself and those children of the night, the wolves."

"And most impressive that was too, Mr Alucard – but no more unusual a relationship, I fancy, than the one that could exist between a wolf-pack and an experienced zoo-keeper. And certainly not one that could be counted as proof that you are a vegetarian vampire."

"Proof? Proof!" Count Alucard fought to keep his voice down as he clambered up on to his gangly legs and stepped out into the aisle of the coach. "Very well! If it is proof that you are seeking, Mr Hetherington, then seeing is believing! Watch this!"

With a quick glance first of all to reassure himself that the other passengers were fast asleep, and also that the coach driver's full attention was on the road ahead, Count Alucard snatched up the hem of his black cloak with both hands, then stretched out his arms on either side of his body. As the old actor stared in wide-eyed, open-mouthed astonishment, the Transylvanian nobleman appeared to shrivel up in front of his face. A moment later, Count Alucard had completely vanished and in his place there was a tiny black, furry-bodied, beady-eyed, blunt-nosed, sharp-eared

creature, hovering on outspread membraneous wings.

"Ouch!" said Harcourt Hetherington, as he pinched his own arm hard to make sure that he wasn't dreaming.

As further proof of its existence, the vegetarian vampire-bat flew all the way down the coach, flitting from side to side, then turned and flitted back as far as the driver's seat, where it hovered for a full three seconds unnoticed over Albert Ridley's cloth-capped head, before returning to the point from whence it had set out. A moment later, Count Alucard had returned himself to human form and was sitting next to Harcourt Hetherington.

"Good heavens above!" gasped the old actor.

"Well, Mr Hetherington?" said Count Alucard. "*Now* do you believe my story?"

"My dear, good fellow, please accept my heartfelt apologies for ever having doubted you," began the actor. "Secondly, allow me to assure you that your secret is safe with me. And if performing as an actor in the Harcourt Hetherington company will help you to evade your pursuers, then I am both pleased and proud for you to stay with us for as long as it is in your interests to do so."

Count Alucard did not reply. It was not often that any member of the human race went out of its way to be kind to him and, when such an occurrence did take place, the count was almost moved to tears. Taking a large white handkerchief with the monogram "C.A." embroidered in one corner out of his pocket, the count blew his nose hard, twice.

"Motorway ahead!" announced Albert Ridley.

The coach driver swung the steering wheel and, followed by the lorry which contained the costumes, props and scenery, moved on to the slip road leading to the motorway. "Here we go then!" added Albert Ridley, over his shoulder. "England, home and beauty – here we come!"

"*England?*" Count Alucard echoed the word in some surprise. He had no idea that this was where they were heading. "England!" he breathed again.

"Why, yes," said Harcourt Hetherington. "It will take us several days to get there. But England is where we play our next engagement."

"England!" And this time, Count Alucard spoke the word softly to himself. He snuggled happily in his seat. England! England was the country where his best friend, Henry Hollins, lived. England was where he kept his second-best coffin, snug and safe in the sitting-room of the Hollins family, at 42, Nicholas Nickleby Close, in Staplewood. He would find some way of visiting the Hollinses, Count Alucard told himself. He was only sorry that he had not been able to write and let them know that he was on his way to see them.

"Never mind," he told himself, as he watched the dawn steal up over the horizon. "It will come as a nice surprise for Mr and Mrs Hollins and Henry."

10

NO MILK, PLEASE, MR MILKMAN, UNTIL FURTHER NOTICE. Emily Hollins read again the words that she had written on the note, folded it carefully, slipped it into the top of the empty milk bottle, then stooped and set the milk bottle down outside the back door of Number 42, Nicholas Nickleby Close.

"That's that job done," said Emily to Albert. "And I've been into the newspaper shop and cancelled all our deliveries until we come back."

"Well done, that woman!" said Albert Hollins, with an approving nod. The last time the Hollins family had gone away, they had forgotten both of the above-mentioned tasks. They had returned from a fortnight's holiday by the sea to discover fourteen bottles of milk cluttering the back porch, together with four large bottles of orange juice and six cartons of yoghurt. They had then been unable to open the door because of the pile of magazines and newspapers on the doormat.

On another memorable occasion, they had come back after a week away to find that Mr Hollins had forgotten to lock the back door when they had left. Their pleasant memories of seven days spent cruising the Norfolk Broads had been dispelled immediately on discovering that the deep-freeze cabinet was empty and the sink was piled high with dirty dishes. The tramp responsible for both of these circumstances was fast asleep and snoring gently in Mr and Mrs Hollins' double bed, his scruffy grey-black beard resting on the duvet.

"A bit like Goldilocks and the three bears," Emily Hollins had observed several days afterwards, when she had recovered from the shock.

"Goldilocks had the good manners, at least, to take to her heels when the three bears came back," Albert Hollins had growled in reply. The tramp had taken up residence in the Hollins' home and refused to leave until Albert Hollins had provided him with an old overcoat and his bus-fare into the centre of Staplewood.

Mr Hollins sniffed at the recollection of his past unpleasant experiences. Then, having assured himself that on this occasion, both the milkman and the newspaper shop had been taken care of and the back door locked securely, he turned his attention towards Henry, who was standing, looking doleful, on the garden path.

"Perk up, Henry!" said Albert Hollins to his son. "It's National Garden Gnome Week! Life can't be all *that* bad!"

"Sorry, dad," said Henry, trying his hardest to look cheerful. But life, as far as Henry Hollins was concerned at that particular moment, couldn't get much worse. First of all, there was the invitation to Alucard Castle, which could not be taken up.

Secondly, there was the whole weekend to be endured, playing carpet bowls with Uncle Jim and Auntie Flo. Lastly, there was the daunting prospect of the journey to his relatives' home – as boring a car-ride as any lad could have wished upon him when travelling on the motorway, but three times as long and nine times more boring when going by the diversionary route chosen by his father, and pausing every now and then to seek out garden gnomes.

"I've put the luggage in the car, Emily," said Albert Hollins, turning to his wife. "But do you have the notepad, clipboard and ballpoint pen handy, to jot down all the gnome-sightings on our outward journey?"

"All present and correct," said Emily Hollins, entering into the spirit of the occasion and patting the large bag that she carried slung on a strap over her shoulder.

"Grand Garden Gnome Hunt – here we come!" announced Albert Hollins. Then, with a cheery goodbye wave at his own gnome collection, dotted around the back garden, he set off towards the family car parked in the drive, followed by Mrs Hollins and a downcast Henry bringing up the rear.

The customs officer at the airport's Arrival counter frowned, slightly puzzled, as he glanced at the unfamiliar double-headed eagle insignia on the covers of the two passports which he had just been handed. He flipped open both of these documents, glanced at the photographs on the inside pages and checked the likenesses of the two men standing in front of him. The faces fitted the photographs. The first of the pair was rather fat, had a pointed moustache, and was dressed in a uniform which carried a row of shiny medals across the chest. The other man was small, wore a badly-fitting suit, and was blinking nervously. The smaller man was holding a big suitcase in both of his hands; the uniformed man was clutching a curious big, black, bulging velvet bag.

"Would you mind telling me, sir, exactly what you have inside that bag?" asked the customs official, whose name was Colin Lightfoot.

In answer, Sergeant Kropotel unfastened the silken cord which secured the bag and then tipped out the contents. The heavy mallet and the several long wooden stakes rattled down on to the counter. Colin Lightfoot picked up one of the stakes and tested its point on the ball of his thumb.

"Ouch!" he went, surprised at its sharpness. "What are they for? Are they tent-pegs? Are you going camping?"

"That is the Official Vampire Destruction Kit of Tolokovin," said Sergeant Kropotel, pulling himself up to his full height and clicking his heels together smartly, causing his medals to jangle against each other. "I am Police Sergeant Alphonse Kropotel, Chief Vampire Hunter of Tolokovin – and this is my assistant, Karl Gustaffe."

"I am only acting as a vampire hunter in a temporary capacity," Gustaffe hastened to explain. "My true profession is that of master baker."

"Did you say 'vampire hunters'?" asked Colin Lightfoot, not showing the slightest interest in Karl Gustaffe's real calling. "And would you mind telling me the purpose of your visit to the United Kingdom? Are you both on your holidays?"

"Certainly not!" snapped Sergeant Kropotel, picking up the wooden stakes one by one and replacing them in the bag. "We are here on an official vampire hunt."

"Vampires?" scoffed the customs officer. "You'll be lucky! Don't be daft! There aren't any vampires in this country."

"I happen to know, for a certain fact," began the Transylvanian policeman importantly, "that Count Alucard – the last of the vampires – has smuggled himself over here."

"Wow!" murmured the customs man, impressed

at the solemnity in Kropotel's voice. "Did you say that this chap's name was Alucard?"

"Count Alucard," replied Kropotel.

"It's 'Dracula' backwards," put in Karl Gustaffe, helpfully.

"A-L-U-C-A-R-D . . ." Colin Lightfoot spelled out the letters softly to himself, and then spelled them out a second time, from back to front: "D-R-A-C-U-L-A . . ." After which, he gulped twice, then continued quickly, "You're right. It is. Would you two mind waiting here for a couple of minutes, while I ask the airport's police inspector to come out and see you? I'm sure he'd like to hear what you've just told me."

As Customs Officer Lightfoot headed hotfoot for the door, the little baker lowered the heavy suitcase down on to the ground. Karl Gustaffe had a feeling that their problems were far from over. Sergeant Kropotel, on the other hand, took a more optimistic view.

"We're getting close to the evil monster, Gustaffe," Kropotel told his assistant as he cradled the bulky velvet bag and ran his fingers, above the cloth, over the sharp-pointed stakes. "He *is* somewhere in England, I *know* he is! And with the help of the authorities here, we will have hammered half a dozen stakes through Alucard's heart before you can say, 'The holy bones of Saint Unfortunato'!"

But the little baker said nothing. He did not have the slightest desire to hammer wooden stakes into the heart of any creature. He had not wanted to come on the vampire hunt in the first place. He had no wish to stay in England. He would be happy when the whole sad, sorry business was over and done with and he was back home in Tolokovin, making goose-liver fancies, shrubel-cakes and mouth-watering goat's meat tarts . . . Karl Gustaffe shuffled his feet and glanced down at the floor as Alphonse Kropotel began to sing an old Transylvanian vampire hunting folk-song softly to himself:

"Sovra zora,
Sovra sofra-hovrey,
Sovra hofra-sofrey,
Sofra, sofra – gluck . . ."

Albert Ridley, the coach driver, had not had the slightest difficulty in driving his passengers from Transylvania through country after country, right across Europe and thence on to the cross channel ferry. Once they were ashore in England, finding the route on to the motorway had been simplicity itself. Nothing could have been easier than driving up the motorway; the trouble was to begin at the very moment that Mr Ridley decided that the time had come to make an exit.

If the coach driver had admitted, there and then, that he had driven off the motorway at the wrong junction, things might not have been quite so bad. But Albert Ridley was not the sort of man who gave up easily, neither was he the kind of chap to own up instantly when he made a mistake. Keeping his error to himself, he drove on, firstly up one country road, then down another, doubling back along a third, passing through several villages and hamlets, jolting over a hump-backed bridge, bumping along a cart-track, down a narrow twisting lane which took him eventually to a roundabout, and then on to another country road.

"Ouch!" grunted Harcourt Hetherington as the coach wheels jarred on the road, after having temporarily risen from the ground. "I do believe that is the second time that we have travelled, none too comfortably, over that very same hump-backed bridge," he complained.

"Now that you come to mention it, Mr Hetherington, I do believe that I have seen that church before," ventured Millie Pilkington, fiddling with her beads with one hand and pointing off across some fields with the other. "I'm sure that I recognise the crooked weather-vane on top of the church spire."

"And I have a feeling that we've passed that public house before," put in Grantley Hardcastle, looking back along the road.

"I don't think so," said Albert Ridley, but with a sinking feeling that the stage-manager was right. "Perhaps we passed another one that looked just like it?"

"It's possible," agreed Grantley Hardcastle, then added, "On the other hand, it's hardly likely that there are two public houses within a mile or two of each other, and both of them called The Frog and Bucket."

At that point, on Harcourt Hetherington's instructions, the coach pulled up on the outskirts of the village they had just driven through.

Moments later, the lorry containing the scenery, props and costumes drew up behind. Several of the passengers peered back the way they had just come. They saw a picture-book collection of thatched cottages with colourful gardens, dotted around a village green which came complete with a parade of ducks; the two proud, greeny-black-brown parents led a string of squawking ducklings waddling towards the duck-pond.

"If you are lost, Mr Ridley, I think it would be best to own up to that fact now," said Harcourt Hetherington, sternly. "We are booked to perform *Murder At Maltravers Hall* this evening. It is important that we arrive at the theatre as quickly as is possible."

"Well, let me put it this way," replied Albert Ridley, having decided that the time had come for him to tell the truth – or something very close to it. "I'm not exactly lost . . . On the other hand, I'm not one hundred per cent certain about where we are, exactly . . ."

"Haven't you got a road map?" said the old actor.

"Haven't I just!" Albert Ridley assured his employer, pointing at a whole stack of well-thumbed maps resting on a shelf underneath the dashboard. On inspection though, it turned out that while there were maps of every highway and byway in every country they had journeyed through in Europe, there was not one single map relating to any part of England. "That's funny," said the coachdriver, removing his cloth cap and scratching his bald head. "I was sure I had one when we set off."

"We *are* lost," groaned the actor Bernard Dugdale, who was sitting near the front of the coach and eavesdropping on the conversation.

"Golly gumdrops!" cried Lucy Lanebury, the youngest member of the company, clapping a hand to her mouth. "We shall miss tonight's performance!"

"Not so long as there is breath left in my body!" a voice cried fiercely. It was Fiona Carlton-Walters (Mrs Harcourt Hetherington, of course) who had spoken, her face appearing over the back of a seat towards the rear of the coach.

The company's leading actress had slept all through the previous night and all of that morning, with the assistance of a black mask over her eyes and the benefit of two whole seats to stretch herself across. Now the anxious voices of her fellow actors had at last disturbed her slumbers. "I have been in the theatrical profession for over thirty years, and I have never missed a performance in my entire life. I do not intend to break that habit now!" The elderly actress rose majestically, to her feet, and swept down the aisle of the coach to confront her husband. "The show must go on!" declared Fiona Carlton-Walters, adding, "Harcourt – something must be done!"

"I know, my precious one," her husband replied with a sigh. "The question is – what?"

"How would it be," proposed Count Alucard, eager to help as always, "if I were to walk back into the village we have just come through,

and find someone able to tell us precisely, where we are, and in which direction we should proceed?"

"Brilliant!" cried Lucy Lanebury, clapping her hands together.

"That seems to make sense," said Grantley Hardcastle.

"Sounds good to me, old chap," agreed Bernard Dugdale.

"Well done, that man!" exclaimed Harcourt Hetherington.

At which point, taking their lead from their employer, several other company members added their own approvals to the count's proposal.

"If it were done when 'tis done," snapped Fiona Carlton-Walters, quoting a line from Shakespeare, "then 'twere well it were done quickly."

"I'll go at once," replied the count. Which is exactly what he did.

⋆

"*Brrr-brrrrr . . . Brrr-brrrrr . . . Brr-brrrrr . . .*" There was a faint "click" as the ringing-tone stopped and then the recorded voice of Henry Hollins could be heard, reading a message which had been written by his father: "Hello! You have reached the home of the Hollins family. I am afraid that we are not available at the moment to take your call, but if you would care to leave your name and number after the bleep, we will get back to you as quickly as we can . . ."

Count Alucard sighed sadly and replaced the telephone on the handset in the village phone-box without saying a word. What was the point of leaving his name, when he did not have a phone number to go with it? This was the third time that day that the count had tried to phone Henry Hollins, and each time without managing to speak to him.

The coach had arrived at Dover on the cross channel ferry early that morning. Count Alucard had made his first unsuccessful phone call not long after, as soon as he had been able to get to a telephone. He had made his second attempt when the company had pulled up for breakfast at a stopping-place on the motorway, and with the same negative result. It was now close to lunchtime and still, it seemed, there was nobody in at the Hollins' home.

"If only I knew where we were," the vegetarian vampire count murmured to himself, as he gnawed anxiously at his lower lip with one of his pointy teeth, "I could leave a message and give Henry *some* idea of my whereabouts . . ." But the trouble was, of course, that neither the count nor any one of his theatrical travelling companions had the slightest idea of their exact location.

Count Alucard glanced through the phone-box window to where the coach was parked, some hundred metres or so away along the lane beyond the village. Suddenly, he felt just a little bit ashamed of himself. He had come into the village to ask the way, and then allowed himself to be diverted from that task by trying to make his phone call. The sight of the public telephone box at the edge of the village green had been too great a temptation. He had not been able to resist one more attempt to phone his dear friend, Henry Hollins.

"And now that I have failed again in that respect," the Transylvanian nobleman told himself, "I must see to it that I succeed in what I first set out to do." Happily, he felt sure that no one on the coach would have noticed that he had allowed himself to be waylaid. Pushing open the door, he stepped out of the phone box and on to the grass verge. Looking up and down the street, he peered into several cottage gardens – but could not see a single person. Considering the time of day, the count decided that the villagers were probably in their kitchens, either sitting down to, or preparing, lunch. He would need to knock on one of the front doors. But which one should he choose.

Count Alucard's eyes roamed over several garden fences, then lingered on a peeling, green-painted wooden door set in a high, ivy-covered, red-brick crumbling wall. While most of the cottage gardens were in full view, the closed green door hinted at secrecy. The Count's mind was made up instantly. There was nothing that the vegetarian vampire liked better than a touch of mystery. In a matter of seconds, his gangly legs had taken him to the door in the wall. He reached out and took a firm hold on the rusting iron ring which acted as a handle. The ring groaned, complainingly, as it turned at his touch – and then the door swung open.

"A vampire?" said Police Inspector Arnold Corcoran, drumming his podgy fingers nervously on his desk-top. "You are asking me to believe, Mr Lightfoot, that a real, live, genuine, blood-sucking monster has succeeded in making its way on to our shores?"

"It's true, Inspector," replied the customs officer, nodding firmly. "These two gentlemen can confirm that awful fact."

The police inspector looked at the two men who were standing, one on either side of the customs officer, on the other side of his desk. The first of them was stockily built, red-faced, had a pointed moustache, and was wearing a curious brown uniform with lots of gold braid. There was a row of medals dangling across his chest and he was clutching a bulky, black drawstring velvet bag up against them. The second man was smaller than his companion and wore a roughly-made suit that seemed just that much too big for him.

"The vampire is called Alucard," said the uniformed man. Then, after clearing his throat noisily, he added, "He is *Count* Alucard. He lives in Castle Alucard, close by the village of Tolokovin, in Transylvania."

" 'Alucard' is 'Dracula' backwards," explained the smaller of the two.

"Is it really?" Chief Inspector Corcoran picked up a pen from his desk, drew forward a notepad and wrote "A-L-U-C-A-R-D" in big letters, then wrote "D-R-A-C-U-L-A" underneath. "Heaven preserve us, Lightfoot!" he gulped, pushing the notepad across the desk. "See for yourself."

"I know, sir. I've tried it out already," said the customs officer, without even bothering to look at what Chief Inspector Corcoran had written. Then, turning to Kropotel, he continued, "Show the inspector what you've got in that bag."

For the second time that day, Alphonse Kropotel unfastened the cord which secured the bag, then tipped out the contents. This time, the heavy mallet and the several carefully crafted stakes spilled out across the police chief's desk.

"Be careful!" snapped the chief inspector as the mallet struck a picture frame which held a photograph of Sybil Corcoran, his wife, standing in the Corcoran conservatory, watering hydrangeas. "I can do without your tent-pegs knocking over my personal belongings, thank you very much!"

"They're not tent-pegs, sir," said Colin Lightfoot.

"They look very much like tent-pegs to me," muttered Arnold Corcoran, as he picked up one of the stakes and then tested its point. "*Ouch*, that's sharp!" he complained, as he watched a small pinpoint of blood ooze out and then swell large on the ball of his thumb.

"That is the Official Vampire Destruction Kit of Tolokovin," put in Sergeant Kropotel, clicking the heels of his smartly polished boots together. "I am Alphonse Kropotel," he added, "Chief Vampire Hunter of Tolokovin – and this is my assistant, Karl Gustaffe."

"I'm a master baker when I'm not vampire hunting," said Kropotel's assistant.

"And are you absolutely sure about this vampire?" asked the chief inspector, after he had carefully licked the spot of blood off his thumb. "Has it really got into this country?"

"Without a doubt," replied Kropotel, twisting one end of his moustache between finger and thumb. "We have followed hard on the monster's heels all across Europe. And he most certainly *is* a vampire, as his father was, and his grandfather before him. All of his ancestors were vampires. And all of them . . ." Alphonse Kropotel paused, picked up the mallet and one of the stakes, then tapped the first against the second significantly. "We know how to deal with vampires in Tolokovin," he added. "It is the only way. If not, they will destroy mankind."

Chief Inspector Arnold Corcoran took out his handkerchief and dabbed at the ball of his thumb while he thought long and hard.

"Don't you think that we should do something quickly, sir?" urged Colin Lightfoot. "Before this vampire starts biting people? If the news gets out that he's here in our midst, there really will be a panic on. I think you ought to take some serious action – before he destroys us all!"

"Don't tell me how to do my job, Lightfoot!" growled the Chief Inspector as he returned the handkerchief to his pocket. "I know how to act with speed, when necessary, without your help. I didn't become a chief inspector by sitting around and doing nothing!" Then, as if to prove his point, Arnold Corcoran reached out and snatched up one of the several telephones which were on his desk. "Put me through to Number Ten, Downing Street, at once," he said. "I want to speak to the Prime Minister immediately."

Colin Lightfoot blinked and raised his eyebrows. Gosh, he thought to himself, that really *was* taking serious action! At the same time, Alphonse Kropotel began to breathe a little more quickly. Things really *were* beginning to happen. His grip tightened on both the mallet and the sharp-pointed stake. Karl Gustaffe rubbed the toe of one of his shoes nervously across the carpet. He wondered whether it wasn't all getting a bit *too* serious. It had suddenly occurred to the little baker that, during all his lifetime, he had never heard of Count Alucard actually biting anyone at all.

"Good morning, Mister Prime Minister, sir," said Arnold Corcoran into the telephone. "Chief Inspector Corcoran here – you may remember that we once met, several years ago, when you very kindly presented the prizes at the Policemen's Sports Day. I was the chap who got the medal for coming second in the sack race. Sorry to bother you when you've got the country to govern, but something rather serious has just cropped up . . ."

11

"Do you really think I ought to, Dad?" asked Henry Hollins, hovering uncertainly halfway along the uneven, overgrown garden path.

"Of course you should, Henry," urged Albert Hollins from the other side of the garden fence, waving his clipboard encouragingly at his son. "Go on, boy! Go on!"

"What do you think, Mum?" asked Henry, looking towards Mrs Hollins. Like her husband, she was standing outside the garden, close by the family car which was parked in a shady country lane.

"If your father says it's all right, Henry, I'm sure there's nothing you need worry about." But there was a note of doubt in Emily's voice which did little to provide Henry with the reassurance he had been seeking.

Up until that moment, the Hollins family's participation in that year's Grand Garden Gnome Hunt had been a great success. Since setting off early that morning, they had steered a course along whichever country road or byway took Albert's fancy, stopping off to peer over garden fences, through privet hedges, across well-trimmed lawns and neatly paved patios, and "logging", on Mr Hollins' clipboard, the descriptions and addresses of any garden gnomes they chanced to espy.

There had been gnomes aplenty: gnomes perched on plastic mushrooms; gnomes beside garden-ponds, fishing rods at the ready; gnomes reading books; gnomes with upraised lanterns in shady corners; industrious gnomes with garden tools in vegetable patches; lazy gnomes, lying on their elbows on tidy lawns, their chins cupped in their chubby hands . . .

Albert Hollins had scribbled away enthusiastically at every sighting, filling sheet after sheet of paper on his clipboard. His enthusiasm was infectious. It was not long before Emily and Henry Hollins had entered into the spirit of the occasion, their voices raised with Albert's as they drove along, trilling a song he had composed:

"*Gnome hunting we will go,*
Gnome hunting we will go,
Eee-Aye-Addy-Oh,
Gnome hunting we will go!"

They had spotted quite a number of similarly enthusiastic gnome hunters on their travels – they had even shared coffee, fizzy orange juice and ginger biscuits with another gnome hunting family, the Appleyards (Mr and Mrs Appleyard and their nine-year-old twin daughters), in a cosy wayside café contained in a retired twelve-seater bus.

Everything had gone swimmingly, and Henry Hollins had been forced to admit to himself that he had thoroughly enjoyed that morning – until they had arrived outside that overgrown garden in the leafy lane.

"Tally ho! Garden gnomes on the starboard bow!" Albert Hollins had shouted, braking the car so hard and fast that Henry had bounced on his seat while Emily's glasses had been jolted down to the tip of her nose. Then, snatching up his clip-board, Mr Hollins had bounded out of the car and peered across the garden fence. He had been joined moments later by Emily and Henry, who found themselves gazing across a large untended stretch of garden – which contained a couple of garden gnomes at least, staring back at them out of the long grass. The garden, which was dotted with stunted trees, went back so far that the house was hidden from view. Albert's sighting of the pair of gnomes had given him cause to wonder whether there might be more of the species, positioned further back in the weed-infested undergrowth.

Which was why Henry Hollins now found himself, alone and trespassing, standing halfway down the mossy garden path. "Supposing someone should come out and see me?" asked Henry anxiously, looking back at where his parents stood on the other side of the garden fence.

"Don't worry, Henry!" called back Mr Hollins. "The occupants here must be garden-gnome lovers too. Just tell them that you're taking part in the Grand Garden Gnome Hunt and they'll be sure to understand. Anyway, in all probability there won't be anyone at home – they'll be out and about like all sensible folk today, taking part in the Hunt themselves. Don't *worry*, son! Just see how many more gnomes you can spot, and let me know their general description."

It's all very well, him telling *me* not to worry, sighed Henry Hollins to himself, as he set off again down the garden path, urged on by his father waving the clipboard, but I'm the one on this side of the garden fence – not Dad.

Some moments later, and to add to his discomfort, Henry realised that a curve in the path had taken him behind a clump of trees and out of his parents' line of sight. Even worse, he was now close to, and thus plainly visible from, the house: a sprawling, slab-stone roofed, centuries-old, unfriendly-looking, ivy-covered building with peeling, green-painted wooden shutters closed tight over every window.

At least the shuttered windows go to prove that what Dad said was right – there's nobody at home, Henry comforted himself, adding, and a good job too!

Then, as Henry continued to gaze at the unwelcoming building, a cloud passed in front of the sun, casting both house and garden into gloomy shadow. A breeze sprang up as if from nowhere, whispering through the leafy hanging branches of an old gnarled willow. As quickly as it had come, the breeze was gone – and house and garden were returned to shadow and eerie silence.

"Ri-*VITT*! . . . Ri-*VITT*!" A big frog hidden in

a clump of grass close by Henry's feet croaked loudly, making him jump. He was startled even more a moment later, when a strangely familiar but totally unexpected voice spoke in his ear.

"Henry Hollins!" said the vegetarian vampire nobleman. "Is it really you?"

"Count Alucard!" cried Henry Hollins, turning in amazement and gazing up into the face of his old friend. "You're the last person I expected to bump into here!"

"My dear Henry, those are the very words that I was about to voice myself!" replied the count, embracing Henry. Then, elbows bent, forearms pointing upwards, he clenched his fists and jumped and down in sheer delight. "What incredible good

luck!" he cried. "What total joy! What exceptional good fortune!"

"Great!" said Henry Hollins.

"Show the Prime Minister what you've brought with you all the way from Transylvania," said Chief Inspector Corcoran, nodding at the black velvet bag.

"This is the Official Vampire Destruction Kit of Tolokovin," said Alphonse Kropotel proudly, as he opened the silken drawstring for the third time that morning, then tipped out the contents over the important-looking papers on the Prime Minister's polished desk-top.

"Goodness gracious!" gasped the Prime Minister, as he picked up one of the sharp-pointed stakes.

Chief Inspector Corcoran, Customs Officer Lightfoot, Sergeant Kropotel and Karl Gustaffe were positioned on one side of the desk, while the Prime Minister and the Home Secretary, a small, balding man who wore a constantly bewildered expression and blinked continually, were sitting on the opposite side. The Prime Minister's private office on the first floor at Number Ten, Downing Street, was a large dark-panelled room with a polished wood floor. There was a marble fireplace and a green-shaded desk lamp which matched the long, green curtains at both sets of windows. The portraits of prime ministers past, contained in ornate gilded frames, gazed down solemnly from all four walls.

"I wouldn't do that, Mr Prime Minister – " began Chief Inspector Corcoran as the Prime Minister made to test the point of the stake on the end of his thumb. But Arnold Corcoran spoke too late.

"Ouch!" said the Prime Minister crossly, then frowned as he watched the tiny globule of blood swell on the ball of his thumb. "I wonder if I might beg a favour of you, Home Secretary?" he added.

"Certainly, Prime Minister," said the Home Secretary, eager to please and blinking several times.

"Would you pop outside and see if you can beg a sticking-plaster from one of the servants?"

"No sooner said than done," murmured the Home Secretary, blinking another two times as he headed for the door. In the corridor outside the private office, the Home Secretary blinked again and nodded at the burly detective constable on duty.

"How-de-doody," murmured Detective Constable Kevin Thoroughgood as the Home Secretary whizzed past. The detective constable was the chief inspector's personal assistant, and had been positioned outside the private office with strict instructions that nobody was to be allowed to interrupt the meeting.

"I'm sorry for this slight delay, gentlemen," said the Prime Minister, holding his bleeding thumb up awkwardly as the door closed behind the Home Secretary, "but my wife made the cushions in here herself, and she'd go crackers if I dripped blood on them."

"No problem, Prime Minister," said Chief Inspector Corcoran, then he clasped his hands behind his back, cleared his throat and stared up at a portrait of a gruff-looking previous prime minister, with mutton-chop whiskers and Victorian clothing, who seemed to be staring down at him.

To pass the time, Alphonse Kropotel, hummed a couple of choruses from the vampire hunting song under his breath; while Karl Gustaffe, to keep his baker's skills in practice, repeated the recipe for shrubel-cake inside his head. The Prime Minister meanwhile, busied himself with some important documents concerning traffic regulations in city centres. Minutes later, when the Home Secretary had returned from his errand and the Prime Minister's thumb was safely encased in sticking-plaster, the meeting continued, almost as if there had not been any break.

"How many people in this country know that there's a vampire on the loose?" asked the Prime Minister.

"No one, sir, apart from those sitting around this table," said Corcoran proudly, then, after nodding towards the door, he added "Oh, and Detective Constable Thoroughgood. Today was supposed to be his day off and he'd arranged to play in a snooker tournament – I had to let him in on the secret, in order to get him to report for duty."

"Hmmmm." The Prime Minister nodded, thoughtfully.

"The question is, Prime Minister," said the Home Secretary, pausing to blink quickly three times then continuing, "whether it is best to keep it a secret between ourselves, and thus avert a national panic, or to make it public knowledge, so that the entire nation can be on its guard?"

"My thoughts exactly, Home Secretary," said the Prime Minister, stroking his sticking-plastered thumb with his free hand. "If we were to keep it a secret," he continued, turning to Arnold Corcoran, "how long would it take to catch the monster?"

"I'm afraid that I can't give you an answer to that question, sir, until we know where we can find the evil brute."

"We should be able to pinpoint his exact position at any moment, Prime Minister," said the Home Secretary. "It's a simple matter of our locating the theatrical company that the vampire's been using as a cover. We have half a dozen men working on that very task, even as we speak."

"And when we are in possession of that information, and we have succeeded in capturing the beast, how long will it take to . . .?" The Prime Minister paused, glanced down at the mallet and the several stakes scattered across his desk, shivered, and then continued, "How many men do you think you'll need, Chief Inspector?"

"The fewer the better, Prime Minister – rather than take too many and arouse suspicion," said Arnold Corcoran, glancing around at his companions inside the room. "In fact, I think we have sufficient for the job already. Myself, Customs Officer Lightfoot, our two Transylvanian vampire hunting friends, and my personal assistant, Kevin Thoroughgood. That's five in all: three to hold the vampire down, one to position the stake over its evil heart, the fifth to strike the fatal blow . . ."

"I think that final honour rightfully belongs to me," said Sergeant Kropotel, drawing himself up to his full height and again clicking his heels together.

"Fair enough," said the Chief Inspector, nodding in agreement.

"I wonder, Chief Inspector, if you would permit me to add another member to your team." The Prime Minister picked up a red telephone. "Would you ask the gentleman who has been waiting in reception to step into my private office?" he said.

Seconds later, the door was thrust open and a stockily built man swaggered into the room. The newcomer was wearing a camouflage uniform, camouflage canvas boots and a camouflage baseball cap. A couple of hand grenades dangled from his belt, together with a leather holster which contained a pearl-handled automatic pistol. His eyes were hidden behind dark glasses.

"Gentlemen," said the Prime Minister, waving a hand at the heavily armed man, "allow me to introduce Captain Ozzie Cummings of the SAS."

"Would you excuse me for a moment," said the Home Secretary as a mobile phone rang in his pocket. He took it out. "Yes?" was all that he said into the mouthpiece. A moment later, his eyelids began to flutter excitedly like butterfly's wings. "We've found out where the Harcourt Hetherington Players are to perform tonight!"

"Let's do the business, boys!" snapped Captain Ozzie Cummings, sticking out his clenched fists, thumbs upraised.

"But you don't know yet what it is that we've got to do," said Karl Gustaffe.

"You can brief me on the way," replied the SAS man with a shrug. "I've got a helicopter standing by."

"I simply cannot comprehend my sheer good fortune!" said Count Alucard, shaking his head in disbelief and clasping Henry Hollins' hands warmly in both of his own for the umpteenth time. "Imagine my bumping into you in this outlandish spot. Why, goodness me! It simply defies credulity completely!"

"I know," agreed Henry Hollins. "I can't believe it either."

But the circumstances behind their unexpected encounter are easy to explain.

Having lost his way on the country roads, the coach driver, Albert Ridley, had pulled up by coincidence a short walk from the spot where Albert Hollins had chosen to park the family car. The Hollinses had been driving willy-nilly around that same area of countryside while taking part in the Grand Garden Gnome Hunt.

Count Alucard, having left his theatrical companions on the coach, had entered the green painted door in the high, brick ivy-covered wall in order to ask directions from the owner of the house. At that same moment, Henry Hollins had gone through the gate in the garden fence on to the overgrown lawn beyond. In fact, the gardens they had both entered happened to be one and the same – the only difference being that, while the count had entered by the door in the wall which led him to the front of the house, Henry Hollins had gone in through the gate which opened on to the sprawling back garden. Count Alucard, having rung the front door bell and received no answer, had wandered round to the back of the house – and bumped into his old friend, Henry Hollins.

The Transylvanian nobleman, well-mannered as always, had allowed his excited schoolboy friend first chance at stammering out his reason for being in the garden.

" . . . And so you see," gulped Henry Hollins after he had blurted out his explanation, "we've been out looking for garden gnomes all morning."

"I recall the pleasure that your father gets from

his collection of the quaint little plastic fellows," said the count.

"He's writing down the details of all the ones we see on a big notepad. After that we're off to Wolverhampton to play carpet bowls with Uncle Jim and Auntie Flo. You can come with us, if you want. We've told them all about you. The last time they came to see us, Uncle Jim hid in your coffin for a joke, to put the wind up Auntie Flo. They'd be gobsmacked if they could actually meet you." Henry Hollins paused to get his breath, and then he added, "Oh, *please*, Count Alucard! Do say you'll come!"

"Alas, my dear young friend, if only I could!" replied the vegetarian vampire, raising his hands in apology and fluttering his long, slim fingers in the air. Count Alucard had given Henry so much of his attention that he had almost forgotten his own reason for having entered the garden. But his travelling companions' predicament came flooding back to him. Hastily, the count outlined his adventures over the past few days.

"You've got the part of the butler in a detective play? In a *real* theatre?" Henry Hollins' eyes bulged in admiration. "Wow! That's brilliant!"

"Well, hardly brilliant, Henry," replied Count Alucard, lowering his glance in modesty. "I've only got one line to say, and I've had difficulty learning those few words. I spend most of the play lying on the drawing-room carpet at Maltravers Hall with a plastic knife between my shoulder blades, pretending to be dead."

"All the same," said Henry, "it can't be easy, having to lie still all that time and not fidget."

"Well . . ." Count Alucard, pleased at the compliment, gave another modest little shrug. "It isn't easy, no – but one *tries*. One does one's best." Then, remembering the urgency of the situation, he continued, "But if I don't find someone soon to put myself and my fellow actors in the right direction, there isn't going to a performance of the play tonight, and that would be a tragedy – "

"Henry!" Albert Hollins' voice drifted through the trees to where Henry and the count were standing. Mr Hollins, concerned at his son's absence, had set out along the garden path with Emily in close attendance, in search of him. "*Henry*!" he called again. "Where have you got to?"

"Here, Dad!" cried Henry. "And have I got a surprise for you!" A moment later, Mr and Mrs Hollins rounded the bend in the path and then pulled up short in blank amazement. "Look who I've found!" said Henry Hollins proudly, as if Count Alucard's presence was all his doing.

"Good morrow, Mr and Mrs Hollins!" called Count Alucard, smiling primly at having given them such a shock.

"Well I never!" gasped Emily Hollins.

"Wonders will never cease!" gulped Albert Hollins, shaking his head in total disbelief, then adding, "Where did you spring from?"

A short time later, Count Alucard had repeated his story, but his good humour at seeing Henry's parents was soon replaced by despair. The count was a man whose spirits rose and fell as quickly as a feather might rise and fall on a gust of wind. " . . . And so, you see, we're lost," sighed the vegetarian vampire, his shoulders drooping as he arrived at the end of his story. "Completely, totally and hopelessly lost . . ." And his shoulders drooped just a little more.

"If that's your only problem, count," began Mr Hollins, hiding a smile at his friend's discomfiture, "then your worries are over."

"How's that, Mr Hollins? Do you mean to tell me that you *know* where we are?"

"Well, not exactly," admitted Albert Hollins. "But I do have a road map in the glove compartment in the car."

"Hurrah!" cried the vegetarian vampire, back in the best of humours. Then, turning his sharp, red-rimmed eyes on each of them in turn, and using a phrase he had learned from his theatrical chums, he added, "Let's get the show on the road."

12

"Fasten your seat-belts!" shouted Captain Ozzie Cummings over his shoulder as he jiggled the joystick. "It's going to be a bumpy ride!"

Four of the men who were sitting in the helicopter behind the SAS officer (Chief Inspector Arnold Corcoran, Customs Officer Colin Lightfoot, Sergeant Alphonse Kropotel and Detective Constable Kevin Thoroughgood) held their breath and glanced down through the open door as the camouflaged military aircraft, hugging the contours of the countryside, was forced to bank and then climb sharply, in order to avoid a steep range of rocky hills which had suddenly loomed up ahead. The sixth member of the vampire hunting party, Karl Gustaffe, had both of his hands gripped tight on the safety straps and both of his eyes shut tight, not daring to look.

The little baker from Tolokovin wished hard that, when he dared to open his eyes again, this whole vampire hunting expedition would prove to be no more than an awful dream, and that he would find himself back in the warmth of his friendly bakehouse, rich with the smell of shrubel-cakes baking in the oven. Karl Gustaffe opened one eye, slowly. It was not a dream – and the ground was a long, long way away.

Ozzie Cummings bellowed over his shoulder and also over the engine's roar, when the helicopter was back on an even course. "When we arrive at the dropping-off zone – "

"What do you mean, 'dropping-off zone'?" the chief inspector shouted back, interrupting Cummings. "I hope you're not suggesting that we're going to go down there on parachutes?"

"Not at all!" replied Captain Cummings, who was piloting the helicopter. "I'll be setting us down on *terra firma*, in a field outside the town we're heading for. 'Dropping-off zone' is a technical term we use in the SAS."

"In which case," yelled Arnold Corcoran, "may I suggest that, henceforth; you stop talking in SAS jargon and stick to expressions that we can all understand?" It had occurred to the police officer that Captain Ozzie Cummings was beginning to take command, a task which Corcoran believed belonged to him alone. He decided to make that fact crystal clear. "If I might just remind you, Captain Cummings," he shouted, "this is a police operation that we're mounting, not an SAS mission. I'm in charge!"

"Not while we're up in the air you're not!" Ozzie Cummings shouted back. "I'm the one piloting this helicopter – and, in any aircraft, the pilot's word is law."

Unable to argue with this last statement, Arnold Corcoran held his silence and sulked quietly to himself. All right, Mr Clever-clogs SAS officer, the chief inspector said inside his head. You're in charge for now, but just you wait until we've got our feet on solid ground and, by jolly jumbo, I'll show you who's boss!

The chief inspector was not the only person at that moment who was talking to himself. Listen to them both, said Karl Gustaffe gloomily inside his head. We haven't even set eyes on the vampire yet, and they're starting to fall out already. What will they be like when things *really* start to happen?

Things *were* happening at that same moment inside Alphonse Kropotel's head. But the Tolokovin police sergeant had not so much as noticed the argument between Corcoran and Cummings. Clutching the black velvet bag, Sergeant Kropotel was imagining himself hammering a sharp-pointed stake into the vampire's evil heart. A grim smile flitted across Alphonse Kropotel's lips as he sang the Transylvanian vampire hunting song under his breath:

> "*Sovra zora,*
> *Sovra sofra-hovrey,*
> *Sovra hofra-sofrey,*
> *Sofra, sofra* – SHLUCK!"

"My dear, dear sir!" boomed Harcourt Hetherington, throwing his arms around Albert Hollins and hugging him hard "You are an angel in disguise, sirrah! A veritable angel sent from heaven!"

Fiona Carlton-Walters, Lucy Lanebury and

several other members of the Harcourt Hetherington company who had followed their employer down from the coach took their cue from his words of praise and applauded Albert Hollins by patting their hands together politely.

The Hollins family, together with Count Alucard, had arrived some moments earlier at the coach parked by the scenery van. The count had introduced his three friends to Harcourt Hetherington, who was now expressing his delight at seeing Albert Hollins' road map.

"Glad to be of assistance," murmured Mr Hollins, unused to the theatrical over-enthusiasm and a shade embarrassed by it. "And now, as you're in such a hurry, if you would care to get back on board your coach and tell your drivers to follow my car, it will be my pleasure to lead the way back to the motorway, where you would appear to have got lost in the first place. Then we'll wave our goodbyes and go our separate ways."

"Separate ways, Mr Hollins?" replied the old actor, peering hard at Albert Hollins from underneath his bushy eyebrows. "Did you say 'separate ways', sirrah?"

"Why, yes," said Albert, flustered. "You have to go on to your theatre in time for tonight's performance, and we must get back to our garden gnome spotting." Then, turning towards Emily and Henry and seeking their approval, he added, "Mustn't we?" But his wife and son stayed silent.

"*Gnome* spotting!" roared Harcourt Hetherington in disbelief, and so loudly that Albert Hollins had to take two steps backward in order to keep his balance. "Did you say 'gnome spotting'? My dear fellow, I wouldn't hear of it. No, you shall be our guests tonight, at our opening performance. Shan't they, my dearest?" he added, turning to Fiona Carlton-Walters.

"Whatever you say, Harcourt," murmured that lady.

"I'm sure that it's extremely generous of you to offer, Mr Hetherington, but – " began Albert Hollins. But he was not allowed to finish the sentence.

"Grantley!" bellowed the old actor, adding, in his best Shakespearian tones, "Attend upon me, sirrah – *quickly*!"

"Yes, Mr Hetherington?" said the stage-manager, arriving on the steps of the coach.

"I want three seats in the front row of the dress circle reserved for tonight's performance, in the name of Hollins.

"Yes, Mr Hetherington, I have made a note of it," replied the stage-manager, jotting down the instructions on a notepad.

"Again, it's very kind of you," said Albert Hollins. "But I'm afraid that it's entirely out of the question. You see, we're on our way to spend the weekend with Henry's Uncle Jim and Auntie Flo, and they'd be terribly disappointed if we – "

"My dear chap, no problem." Again Harcourt Hetherington cut short Albert Hollins" objections. "Give your relatives a phone-call, tell them to hop into their car and tootle along to the theatre – we'll take care of them as well. Grantley!"

"Yes, Mr Hetherington?" said the stage-manager, again reaching into his pocket for his notepad.

"'Make that five seats, rather than three, in the dress circle tonight – or, better still, arrange for a box to be placed at our friends' disposal. Oh, and see to it that they are given complimentary drinks and nibbles in the interval."

"Shall be done, Mr Hetherington."

"But – but – but – " stammered Albert Hollins, with another look at Emily and Henry as he attemped to voice his objections for a second time. Again his wife and his son stayed silent.

"Let us not tarry longer thus!" boomed Harcourt Hetherington as he ushered his actors back on to the coach. Then, turning to Count Alucard, he added, "Well, Mr Alucard, are you not joining us?"

"If it's all the same to you, sir," replied the count, edging closer to the Hollinses, "I'll travel with my friends. It's been so long since I saw them – there is so much that we have to talk about."

"As you wish," replied the old actor with a smile. "See you at the theatre."

"Well now! What about that for an unexpected surprise, then?" said Emily Hollins, sitting in the front seat of the car, the open road map on her lap, and addressing Henry over her shoulder. "A night at the theatre – as guests of the star of the show, no less. What a treat!"

"I suppose that's why you didn't back me up when I tried to tell him that it wasn't convenient," said Albert Hollins, crouched grumpily behind the steering wheel, as he drove the car along the motorway. "You knew very well that I wanted to get back on the garden gnome trail."

"It might not have been convenient for *you*, Albert," said Emily, turning her head towards Henry and the count, who were sitting in the back of the car, and giving them a little wink. "But it's *most* convenient for me – I'm *really* looking forward to tonight. And Uncle Jim and Auntie Flo are looking forward to it too." A brief halt had been called for the convoy some minutes before outside a phone-box, in order that Emily might relay the glad tidings to her sister in Wolverhampton. "Flo was lost for words when I told her that we'd be sitting in a box," continued Emily. "And Uncle Jim was over the moon when I told him about the free drinks and nibbles in the interval. It seems to me, Albert . . ." Emily Hollins paused and shot her husband a little frown, "It seems to me that you're the only one who *isn't* looking forward to tonight."

It was Albert Hollins' turn to hold his tongue. He was beginning to feel just a little bit ashamed of himself. He tried to concentrate his attention on the road ahead.

"I'll tell you what I'm looking forward to the most," said Henry Hollins, breaking the awkward silence, "and that's watching Count Alucard playing the butler's part in the play."

"Oh, *please*!" his friend protested, lowering his eyelids and throwing up his pale, slim hands in mock embarrassment. "It's really only the tiniest-*teeniest* role imaginable. I haven't even got my name in the programme. Mr Harcourt Hetherington is the one who brings the audiences flocking in."

"Well, I'm looking forward to seeing *you*," repeated Henry.

"And so am I," said Emily and, as she spoke, she nudged her husband firmly in the ribs.

"Ditto," said Albert, taking Emily's hint and not wishing to hurt Count Alucard's feelings. "I can hardly wait," he added.

"You are all much, *much* too kind," said the count, basking in the Hollinses' enthusiasm. "And, in return, may I humbly state that it will give *me* the utmost pleasure to perform for you."

They were all four agreed that an exciting night lay in store for them – but exactly *how* exciting a night it would prove to be, they had yet to learn. . . .

"I thought that the first act went very well, *very* well indeed," observed Karl Gustaffe, as he sipped at his glass of orange juice during the interval, in the stalls bar of the small provincial theatre. "Even better than when we saw it before in Transylvania," he added, looking at Sergeant Kropotel.

Due to an error in their calculations (Captain Cummings had blamed Chief Inspector Corcoran's chart-reading abilities, while the chief inspector had insisted that it was the SAS officer's piloting skills that were at fault) the helicopter had put down some way from their intended 'dropping-off zone' and consequently, they had not arrived at the theatre until after the curtain had gone up. Having tiptoed to their seats, trying not to disturb the audience, the six members of the vampire hunting party had contented themselves with watching the first act of *Murder At Maltravers Hall*. Now, in the interval, four of them were waiting in the bar while their two senior officers had gone off to reconnoitre the theatre and thus plan the operation.

"And to give him his due," continued the little baker, "I thought that Count Alucard was *very* good tonight. Even though he didn't have a great deal to do, he looked like a real butler."

"Fiddlesticks, you stupid shrubel-cake maker!" sneered Kropotel, shifting the bulky black velvet bag from underneath his left arm to underneath his right. "He looked exactly like himself – a Transylvanian blood-drinking monster – and the sooner I hammer a stake into his evil heart, the sooner the children of Tolokovin shall sleep easier in their cots."

"Sshhhh!" Detective Constable Thoroughgood hissed at the two Tolokovinites. "Stop talking about Transylvania and blood-sucking vampires in here. You'll start a panic."

"He's right," agreed Colin Lightfoot, glancing anxiously around the bar. "And do keep your voices down. We're an odd-looking bunch as it is, without attracting more attention to ourselves."

The customs officer was right. They *were* an 'odd-looking bunch', drawing curious glances already from several of the theatre-goers mingling in the stalls bar.

Firstly, and in order of rank, there was Customs Officer Lightfoot himself, dressed in his smart black uniform, with his white-topped hat and gold-

buttoned jacket. Secondly, there was Sergeant Alphonse Kropotel, wearing his Transylvanian policeman's gold-braided uniform, with a row of medals across his chest and his trouser legs tucked into his calf-length shiny black boots. Next there was Detective Constable Kevin Thoroughgood, who did not wear a uniform, but who looked as if he had been squeezed into his dark-brown suit and who was big enough to stand out in any crowd. Lastly, and with no official rank at all, there was Karl Gustaffe – baker by trade, but vampire hunter by appointment – who, contrasting with Kevin Thoroughgood, was so small that all of his home-spun, roughly tailored clothes appeared to be two sizes too big for him.

Yet if the four above-named men could be described as an "odd-looking bunch", they were soon to become even odder-looking, when they were joined by the two senior officers already elbowing their way towards them across the bar. Chief Inspector Arnold Corcoran was formally dressed in a neat black suit, a white shirt with a dark-blue, white-spotted tie and a bowler hat – while Captain Ozzie Cummings of the SAS was dressed in his camouflage jacket and trousers, and his camouflage canvas boots. He had had the good sense, at least, to take the hand-grenades off his belt and tuck them out of sight in his trouser pockets, so as not to alarm the theatre-goers.

"How goes it, sir?" asked Kevin Thoroughgood, as his superior officer approached the bar with the SAS man in close attendance.

In answer, Chief Inspector Arnold Corcoran pressed a forefinger to his lips, while Captain Ozzie Cummings beckoned them all towards a quiet corner of the bar, away from possible eavesdroppers. Since leaving the helicopter, the police inspector and the SAS officer had had a little chat. They had decided to sink their differences, for the time being at least, and work together in order to best bring about the end of their common enemy: the Transylvanian vampire.

"Now then, lads," began Arnold Corcoran, once the six vampire hunters were seated around a table, "Captain Cummings and myself have had a good look round. We've studied the layout of the theatre and, before we go back in to watch the rest of the play, we're going to fill you in on our plan of attack."

"Pay attention," said Ozzie Cummings, sharing the command. "Here's how we're going to nobble the bloodsucking brute."

Henry Hollins licked the little plastic spoon, put it in his empty ice-cream tub and placed it carefully underneath his chair. The free drinks and nibbles during the interval, in the circle bar, had been voted a treat. The Hollins party were back in their complimentary seats in the box.

"I scream, you scream, we all scream for ice-cream," joked Uncle Jim, giving Auntie Flo a wink as he licked a last tiny sliver of chocolate from off his choc-ice wrapper, then squeezed the silver foil into a tight little ball and made as if to throw it over the box and into the stalls below.

"Jim Tunnicliffe!" gasped Emily Hollins, in shocked surprise. "Don't you dare!"

"Oh, pay no attention to him, Emily," said Auntie Flo with a smile. "He wouldn't throw it in a million years. He's trying to be funny. You know what he's like." And, as if to prove her point, she leaned across, took the wedge of foil from out of her husband's hand and got rid of it, tidily, in one of the empty ice-cream cartons.

"This is the life!" announced Uncle Jim, winking again, this time in Emily's direction. Then, taking a packet of boiled sweets from his pocket, he proffered them around. "Gob-stopper, anyone?" he said.

It certainly *was* the life. They were all four agreed on that. Henry Hollins, who had never sat in a theatre box before, wriggled in the comfort of his chair, which had a padded seat and back and gold-painted arm-rests and legs. He glanced up towards the ornate, gilded ceiling where a huge chandelier, with countless lights contained behind shimmering cut-glass pendants, hung down over the auditorium. Henry, leaning forward, rested his chin on his folded arms and peered down into the stalls. The first few theatre-goers, drifting back from the bar, were heading towards their seats. Henry Hollins realised that the interval would soon be over. He had enjoyed the first act enormously (although he had been surprised at how little Count Alucard had had to do) and wondered what was going to happen in the second half of the play.

But as Henry pondered on the events which were about to happen on the stage, something caught his attention in the stalls below. He frowned, stared hard, blinked twice and then stared hard again. "*Dad?*" He turned and whispered at his father. Albert Hollins, intent on unwrapping a boiled sweet, did not hear his son. "*Dad!*" Henry hissed again.

At that exact same moment, the lights began to dim on the glittering chandelier that hung above the stalls and, seconds later, the curtain rose on Act Two, Scene One of *Murder At Maltravers Hall.* The plot was about to thicken – not only in the world of make-believe on-stage, but also in real life.

*

"*Miaooo*-OWWW!"

Detective Constable Kevin Thoroughgood jumped with fright as an alley-cat yelled out behind him in the dark. He had unintentionally stepped back on the poor animal's tail and it shot off, still howling, between his feet and along the back-street. The big policeman shivered and tried to pull himself together. Despite his size, Constable Thoroughgood was never completely at ease on duty, late at night, in gloomy dark alleys.

"It isn't fair," Kevin Thoroughgood grumbled to himself as he stood outside the stage-door of the theatre. "Why should those others get to see the rest of the play, while I'm stuck out here for the whole of the second act?"

But Detective Constable Thoroughgood was not the only member of the vampire hunting party to have been denied the pleasure of watching the second half of *Murder At Maltravers Hall.* Just around the corner, at the end of the stage-door alley, was the theatre's public entrance. Here Colin Lightfoot, the customs officer, was also doing guard duty. The positioning of these two men outside the theatre had been part and parcel of the plan drawn up by Chief Inspector Corcoran and Captain Cummings during their reconnoitre in the interval.

Having discovered that the stage-door and the front entrance were the only means of exit from the theatre, Corcoran and Cummings had decided that, if these two avenues of escape were well guarded, then the vampire would remain trapped within. Having thus ensured that the monster could not get away, the next step had been to decide upon the manner in which they would secure the evil creature's capture.

The second stage of the operation, although simple, seemed a foolproof plan. With both exits guarded, Corcoran, Cummings and the two Transylvanian vampire hunters could afford to bide their time throughout the second act of the play. It had been decided that these four would remain in their seats until the play had ended and the actors had taken their curtain calls. Then, as the curtain fell for the final time, and as the audience moved out up the aisles towards the rear of the stalls, the four vampire hunters would head with all speed in the opposite direction. With Captain Cummings at their head, the four would rush through the pass-door at the front of the stalls, which would take them from the auditorium into the backstage area. They would burst into Count Alucard's dressing-room before he had even begun to remove his make-up. It would prove an easy task for the four of them to pin the Transylvanian vampire to the ground. Then, while Corcoran, Cummings and Kropotel held the vampire down, it was to be Karl Gustaffe's duty to sound off the theatre's fire-alarm.

"When you hear the alarm bell ringing," Chief Inspector Corcoran had instructed Throughgood and Lightfoot during the interval, at a whispered briefing around the stalls bar table, "you will proceed with all speed to the vampire's dressing-room."

"When we are all assembled, and with the

vampire pinned down securely, the rest will be easy," Ozzie Cummings had continued, smiling grimly at the bulky black velvet bag on Sergeant Kropotel's lap. "Are there any questions?"

"I've got a question, sir," Colin Lightfoot had said, raising a tentative hand into the air.

"Ask away."

"This vampire, sir? Supposing, while we're trying to thump the wooden stake into his heart – well, supposing he takes it into his head to change himself into a blood-drinking bat? Wouldn't that make things difficult? I mean to say, sir, holding down a human being is one thing, but trying to get a grip on a squirming, wriggling spooky bat . . . *Ugh*!" The customs officer pulled a face and shivered.

Chief Inspector Corcoran and Captain Cummings exchanged an uneasy glance at the point. It was a possibility that had not occurred to either of them.

"I think I can relieve your worries on that matter," Sergeant Kropotel had said. "Count Alucard will not be able to turn himself into a bat, not while there are lights on in the dressing-room. In common with all vampires, the count needs darkness in order to make use of his evil powers."

On hearing which, the chief inspector, the SAS officer, the detective constable and the customs man had heaved a concerted sigh of relief. Sergeant Kropotel, they reminded themselves, was a Transylvanian with a great deal of experience in all things to do with vampires.

"Problem solved then," Ozzie Cummings had

said, giving his comrades his usual thumbs-up sign. "But we must see to it that we overpower him quickly when we burst into his dressing-room, before he gets a chance to switch off the lights."

"Is everybody clear, then, about what they have to do?" Chief Inspector Corcoran had asked, and each of them in turn had nodded – with the exception of Karl Gustaffe who, unnoticed by the others, had let out a little sigh and allowed his shoulders to droop. Not long after that, a bell had rung in the stalls bar, summoning the patrons back to their seats. The second act of *Murder at Maltravers Hall* was about to begin.

An hour or so later, outside the stage-door, in the dark of the back-alley, Detective Constable Kevin Thoroughgood glanced nervously over his shoulder as, in his head, he went over his own role in the plan to capture and kill the vampire. He also crossed his fingers and wished, as hard as he could, that the Transylvanian count would not attempt to make a break for freedom before the curtain fell – for surely the spot where he was standing now was dark enough for the evil creature to turn himself into a blood-drinking vampire-bat . . .?

Happily, and much to Thoroughgood's relief, he heard a burst of loud applause coming from inside the theatre, and signalling surely that the play was coming to an end?

Around the corner from the alley, outside the theatre's entrance, Colin Lightfoot had also heard the clapping and the cheers from the auditorium and he too had realised that his ordeal was almost over. Taking a tight grip on the rolled umbrella which he had borrowed as a makeshift truncheon from an umbrella stand inside the foyer, he took a firm stance on the theatre steps and waited for the audience to emerge. Sharing similar feelings to his detective constable comrade, Lightfoot hoped and prayed that he would not encounter, in the rush, a tall, gangly, pale-faced man with long black hair and pointy teeth.

13

"Well done!" 'Bravo!" Hurrah! Hurrah!"

The shouted congratulations mingled with the cheers as the audience rose to their feet as one, and the applause echoed around the ears of the painted cherubs on the theatre's vaulted ceiling. Bathed in the warm glow of the footlights, Harcourt Hetherington hugged centre-stage, with Fiona Carlton-Walters holding his left hand, and Lucy Lanebury grasping his right, while the other actors and actresses were ranged on either side. The company bowed, and bowed, and bowed again – and not one of them bowed lower or prouder than the tall, pale-faced, pointy-toothed butler on the very end, acknowledging the magnificent and well-deserved reception.

Also, it can be stated that the loudest and longest applause came from the box close by the stage which was occupied by the Hollins party. "Good stuff!" cried Uncle Jim, while Auntie Flo and Mrs Hollins clapped until their hands were aching. Oddly enough, though, the chairs which had been occupied by Mr Hollins and Henry both stood empty.

At last, the cheering ebbed away. The Harcourt

Hetherington Players took their last bow of the night and the curtain began to slowly fall. The audience recovered hats and bags and other belongings from under seats, then shuffled into the aisles and headed, in a growing swell, towards the exit doors at the rear. Captain Ozzie Cummings of the SAS, sitting in Row J of the stalls, with his companions on either side, waited until the rows of seats in front of him were clear before making any move.

"Follow me, men!" cried the brave captain, clambering over the empty seat in front of him, and beckoning at the others to follow in his wake. With Kropotel and Gustaffe close behind, and the heavily-built chief inspector making slower progress, the SAS officer clambered over row after row of seats until he arrived at the front of the stalls. "Come on!" he yelled and, in no time at all, the vampire hunters were through the pass-door at the side of the stage and elbowing their way through a gang of stage-hands.

"Excuse me, gentlemen," said Grantley Hardcastle, the stage-manager, moving forward to bar the progress of these intruders. "Company members only allowed backstage."

But the vampire hunters had come prepared for such a contingency. "Police!" snapped Chief Inspector Corcoran, confronting the stage-manager and waving a search warrant in his face. "We are here on official business, and I must ask you to step aside!" Bowing to authority, Grantley Hardcastle was obliged to allow them to pass.

The vampire hunters sped onwards, their footsteps clattering on a spiral flight of iron-cast stairs which took them down a narrow, stone-floored corridor, lined with doors to the actors' dressing-rooms. Captain Cummings, leading the way, ran past the doors marked with golden stars which were reserved for the leading actors, racing on to a dingy door at the very end of the corridor. A small card pinned there, with letters written in felt-tip pen, revealed that the dressing-room belonged to the man they were seeking:

MR C. ALUCARD

Ozzie Cummings placed a forefinger to his lips, warning the others close behind to proceed with caution. He placed an ear to the keyhole.

"We've got him!" he whispered over his shoulder. Then, turning his gaze on Kropotel, he added, "Are you ready to do the business?"

Alphonse Kropotel nodded as he untied the cord on the black velvet bag and his fingers groped inside. Karl Gustaffe stared, and shivered slightly, as Kropotel's hand emerged holding the mallet. He placed it under his left armpit as he plunged his hand back into the bag and felt for a sharp-pointed stake.

"Don't stand there shaking, man," growled Chief Inspector Corcoran at the little baker. "You've got a job to do. I hope you know what it is?"

Karl Gustaffe, pulling himself together, nodded. Dragging his eyes away from Sergeant Kropotel, he glanced back along the corridor at the fire-alarm button behind a small plate of glass on the wall.

Gustaffe noticed that there were several onlookers gathered at the far end of the corridor; the stage-hands they had brushed past earlier had followed them out of interest, and they had been joined by several of the actors and actresses who had come out to see what was going on.

"Would someone kindly inform me as to what is happening?" demanded Harcourt Hetherington, appearing at the door of the Number One Dressing-Room. He was wearing a blue silk dressing-gown, and had a matching silk cravat knotted loosely at his throat.

"I am Chief Inspector Corcoran, sir, and this is Captain Cummings, and these are two of our associates," said the police officer, turning in his direction. "And I must ask you not to interfere with or hamper us in the course of our duties. We have reason to believe that there is a Transylvanian vampire in this dressing-room."

"A vampire? In my company? Without my knowledge?" cried the old actor. "What absolute piffle!"

"Whether you are aware or unaware of the vampire's presence, sir, is an entirely different matter," said Arnold Corcoran sternly. "And one that will need to be considered very carefully when – "

"We can't stand out here in the corridor arguing," Ozzie Cummings broke in. He was a man who preferred actions to words. Placing a shoulder against the door, he gave a mighty push. The dressing-room door flew open. Then, raising his right hand over his head, the SAS man brought it down sharply, crying, "Let's GET HIM!"

The white-faced, pointy-toothed figure seated in the glare of lights surrounding the dressing-room mirror turned in surprise as the vampire hunters burst into the tiny dressing-room.

"Don't move!" commanded Captain Cummings.

"Keep still!" ordered Chief Inspector Arnold Corcoran.

"Prepare to meet your doom!" snarled Sergeant Alphonse Kropotel.

DrrrrING-DrrrrING-DrrrrING-DrrrrING . . .

While all this was happening, Karl Gustaffe had run down the corridor, snatched up the metal hammer on the chain beside the fire-alarm and smashed the glass panel, setting off the alarm. As the bell rang out unceasingly, the actors and stage-hands gathered at the far end of the corridor and began to edge forward, led by the distinguished figure of Harcourt Hetherington, their curiosity increasing.

Inside the dressing-room, Ozzie Cummings had seized the vampire's right hand, while Arnold Corcoran had taken hold of his left. Alphonse Kropotel, mallet in one hand and sharp-pointed stake in the other, stood poised and ready to perform the grim task he had travelled so many miles to carry out. And, all the while, the fire alarm rang on and on and on: *DrrrrING-DrrrrING-DrrrrING-DrrrrING* . . .

"Stop! Stop, I say!" cried Harcourt Hetherington, arriving at the dressing-room door. "Desist from this outrage instantly!"

But it was not the old actor's authoritative

command that made Alphonse Kropotel think twice before striking the deadly blow – it was the pleading voice of his fellow townsman, Karl Gustaffe, that caused the vampire hunter to stay his hand.

"Don't! Don't do it, Sergeant Kropotel!" cried Gustaffe. "That's not the count! You're killing an innocent man!"

"Not Count Alucard?" replied Kropotel doubtfully, weighing the mallet in his hand. "Of course it is! I know a vampire when I see one."

"Count Alucard is much taller than that man, Sergeant," said the baker firmly. "And he's much, *much* thinner too."

"Hold your tongue, you miserable dabbler in dough," growled the police sergeant, as he tried again to position the sharp-pointed stake over his victim's chest, while the chief inspector and the SAS captain did their best to hold the struggling figure still. "Can't you see that I've got work to do?" added Kropotel.

All the same, he was forced to admit to himself that his assistant *did* have a point. The vampire who dwelled in Alucard Castle, high on the mountainside above the village where he had been born, *was* a leaner, taller person than the man wriggling now in front of his eyes . . . "It doesn't matter whether it's Count Alucard or not, Gustaffe," the police sergeant said at last, raising both stake and mallet again. "It's still a vampire, of one kind or another – look at the pale complexion and pointy teeth."

"Of course it isn't a vampire, you foolish fellow,"

snapped Harcourt Hetherington, striding across the room. Then, picking up a face-cloth from the dressing-table, he wiped it over the figure's face. A patch of white cream came off instantly, revealing a healthy-looking human cheek. "Don't you know theatrical make-up when you see it? Or a fake vampire's plastic choppers?" With which, the old actor put his fingers into the figure's mouth and removed a pair of imitation vampire teeth.

Sergeant Kropotel's mouth dropped open.

"You'll oblige me, sirs, by letting that gentleman go instantly," continued Harcourt Hetherington, turning to the chief inspector and the SAS captain. They did as he had told them.

"But if this isn't the vampire we've been chasing," asked Arnold Corcoran with a puzzled frown, "who is it?"

"Hello, Dad," said Henry Hollins, pushing his way into the dressing-room through the actors, actresses and stage-hands peering in at the door.

"Hello, Henry," said Albert Hollins, wiping off more of the make-up from his face. "You took your time getting here. I might have had a sharp-pointed stake hammered into my heart, if it hadn't been for the help of these gentlemen," and Mr Hollins nodded at Karl Gustaffe and Harcourt Hetherington.

"Sorry, Dad," said Henry, with an apologetic shrug. "But it took me *ages* to wriggle my way in here – there's quite a crowd out in that corridor."

"You can say that again, young man," said Colin Lightfoot, following Henry into the dressing-room.

"Are we in time?" asked Detective Constable

Thoroughgood, close on the heels of the customs man. "Have you managed to kill the vampire yet?"

"There isn't any vampire," snapped Ozzie Cummings, crossly. "That is to say, there isn't a *real* vampire." He paused and nodded at Mr Hollins who, by this time, had managed to get most of the make-up off his face. "It was just this fellow dressed up as one."

"What I fail to understand," began Chief Inspector Corcoran, who had been going over the evening's events in his head, in true detective-like fashion, "is why this man was dressed up like a vampire anyway? I thought this was a mystery play and he was supposed to be the butler?"

"That's true!" cried Ozzie Cummings, turning back to Albert Hollins.

"Well . . ." began Albert Hollins then, not knowing what to say next, he put his hand to his mouth and pretended to suffer a bout of coughing. Luckily for Mr Hollins, something happened at that moment to take the attention away from him.

DrrrrING-DrrrrING-DrrrrING-Drrrr – The fire-alarm in the corridor, which had been ringing continuously ever since Karl Gustaffe had set it off, was suddenly silent. Somebody had switched it off.

Fire Station Officer Leonard Wellbeloved, wearing shiny oilskins, a yellow helmet, black rubber boots, and carrying a gleaming axe, pushed his way through the throng at the door and stomped into the already crowded dressing-room. The station officer was *very* angry. He tapped the toe of his left boot on the floor, impatiently, and looked at all of the occupants, one by one.

"Somebody," said Leonard Wellbeloved at last, "has seen fit to authorise the setting-off of this theatre's fire-alarm – despite the fact that the theatre isn't on fire. I have two fire-engines parked outside and twenty firemen twiddling their thumbs, brought here on a wild goose chase. What I want to know is, who's responsible?"

Chief Inspector Corcoran scratched his nose and looked down at the floor. Captain Cummings dug his hands deep in the pockets of his camouflaged trousers, fiddled with the hand-grenades he had previously put there, and tried to look innocent. Detective Constable Thoroughgood coughed twice and shuffled his feet. Customs Officer Lightfoot cleared his throat and looked up at the ceiling. Sergeant Kropotel fiddled with the cord on the black velvet bag and tried to look busy. Karl Gustaffe (who, after all, was guilty only of doing what he had been told to do) edged for the door, hoping his exit would go unnoticed.

"Well?" said Station Officer Wellbeloved. "I'm still waiting."

But nobody in the room, it seemed, could provide an answer to the fire officer's question – or, if they could, they were keeping it strictly to themselves.

"It's been a funny sort of a day all round," reflected Albert Hollins, some time later, after both the vampire hunters and the fire-engines had left, never to return. "It started off with a garden gnome hunt, and then ended up with me being hunted down myself! I'll tell you this much," he added, "there were a couple of moments, when that chap in the Transylvanian police sergeant's uniform was waving the sharpened stake in my face, which made me begin to wonder whether my time was up."

"I wish I could have been here to see him do it," said Emily Hollins, firmly. "I would have given him a piece of my mind! It would have been a long time before he'd have dared to wave sharpened sticks at anyone again." Mrs Hollins, together with Auntie Flo and Uncle Jim, had made their way back stage, after the audience had left, and joined Albert and Henry in the dressing-room. "Who do you say he is?" she added.

"He's Sergeant Kropotel, Mum, and he's the Tolokovin policeman," said Henry Hollins. "You must have seen him swaggering around the village whenever we've been to stay at Alucard Castle. I'd recognise him anywhere."

"It was extremely fortunate that you recognised him tonight, young man, as he returned to his seat in the stalls during the interval," said Harcourt Hetherington, patting Henry on the head. "And it was clever of you, too, to bring your father round to the stage-door, in order for him to take over the butler's role at the curtain call, and thus allow Count Alucard the opportunity to escape."

"I must say, Albert," said Auntie Flo enthusiastically, "you did take your bows well!"

"Hear, hear!" said Uncle Jim, as he mimed clapping his hands together. "I certainly didn't recognise you, old chap – you looked just like a proper actor."

"Thank you, Jim," said Mr Hollins, looking modest. "Although I'm not entirely without theatrical experience. I have appeared on more than one occasion in the Staplewood Garden Gnome Factory Amateur Dramatic Society's Christmas productions. I was a pirate once, in *Treasure Island*, and I also played the part of a weasel in *The Wind in the Willows*."

"But you didn't have any words to say, Albert, on either of those occasions," said Emily Hollins.

"He didn't have any words to say tonight, Mum, either," said Henry Hollins. "All Dad had to do was bow."

"Even so, Henry, your father bowed like a true professional," said Harcourt Hetherington. "Although, of course, he had the kind assistance of Miss Pilkington, our wardrobe mistress, both with his costume and his make-up. It would not do to forget that Miss Pilkington's expertise had a great deal to do with Mr Hollins' success in portraying a Transylvanian vampire appearing as a butler." The old actor paused, wrinkled his brow, and then continued, "Incidentally, speaking of Count Alucard – where has the dear chap got to? I haven't set eyes on him since the kerfuffle with the vampire hunters started."

"I think I know where we might find him," replied Henry, with a knowing little smile. "Much as I like the count, I would be the first to admit that he's not the bravest of vampires. He's probably still hiding. I might know where. Has anybody got a torch?"

"Count Alucard? Count Alucard!" cried Henry Hollins, flashing the sharp, pencil beam of torch-light into the dark above his head. "Can you hear me? If you're up there, Count, it's safe to come down!"

Albert, Emily and Henry Hollins, together with Harcourt Hetherington, Uncle Jim and Auntie Flo, were standing on the darkened stage of the empty theatre, gazing out into the auditorium as the torch-beam picked out a rosy-cheeked painted cherub, perched on a painted cloud, high on the ornate ceiling. Moving the torch a fraction, Henry brought the beam to rest on the splendid crystal chandelier. Hanging upside-down from one of the lower crystal pendants was a small, dark, snub-nosed creature, its membraneous wings wrapped close around its furry body.

"He *is* there!" cried Henry, with delight. "Oh great! I *knew* he would be." Then, raising his voice, he called, "Count Alucard! It's me! It's Henry! It's all right! You can come down! The vampire hunters have gone! *Truly*!"

Just for a moment, it seemed as if the tiny creature was fast asleep and had not heard. Then, all at once and like some large chrysalis blessed with life, the fruit-bat stirred, shook itself, unfurled its wings, released its claws from the chandelier and fluttered off. Several crystal-glass pendants brushed against each other, making a tinkling

sound which seemed to echo around the empty auditorium, before drifting down to the ears of the people standing on stage.

The small winged creature, relishing the space and darkness, zapped all around the upper circle and zoomed close by the cherubs on the ceiling before spiralling down to hover gently just above the stage, face to face with Henry Hollins. Then, as Uncle Jim and Auntie Flo watched in wide-eyed wonder (for they had not seen it happen before) the fruit-bat seemed to shimmer and shake and grow; a moment later, in the pale glow cast by the outer reaches of the torch, the transformation was complete. Count Alucard was standing before them.

"Greetings," said the Transylvanian nobleman. Then, taking hold of Auntie Flo's right hand in his slim fingers, he brushed his lips across her knuckles. "My dear, *dear* lady," he murmured. "May I say what an absolute joy it is to meet you after all this long time? Emily has spoken of you kindly on so many occasions."

"Well, I'm blessed," gasped Auntie Flo.

For once in his life, Uncle Jim was at a total loss for words.

While all this was happening, Harcourt Hetherington had crossed to a control panel in the wings and pressed a button which had turned on a single lamp, used normally for rehearsals, bathing the stage in light but leaving the auditorium in darkness.

"I don't think I would stay here *too* long," the old actor advised on his return. "Although the vampire hunters have disbanded, the fire officer will put in a report. We cannot know which official nosey-parker might turn up next." Harcourt Hetherington paused, pushed back his long white hair, then took hold of Count Alucard's hands in both of his own. "It has been a joy to have met you, my friend, and a pleasure to have enjoyed your talents in the Harcourt Hetherington company of actors – but, sadly, I think the time has come for you to take your leave."

"The story of my life," Count Alucard sighed as a tear appeared in the corner of one red-rimmed eye. "Just when I feel I have found new friends and known true kindness, Fate decrees I must be on my way. It is a lonely life that I am forced to lead . . ." And as he spoke, the tear welled out and crept, slowly, down his cheek.

"Never mind, Count," urged Henry Hollins, smiling up at his Transylvanian friend. "You still have us – we'll take you home. And, don't forget, we've still got your second-best coffin in our sitting-room."

"Of course!" Count Alucard's mood changed instantly. "I haven't enjoyed a good night's sleep for simply ages."

"I suppose that puts the kybosh on the weekend, as far as Flo and yours truly are concerned?" said Uncle Jim to Albert Hollins. "You won't be coming to Wolverhampton after all?"

"How would it be," replied Mr Hollins, "if, instead of us coming to Wolverhampton, you and Flo came back with us to Staplewood?"

"Fantastic!" cried Uncle Jim. "We could have a knock out pairs carpet bowls competition in your sitting-room. Luckily, by chance, I popped the bowls in the boot of the car before we left."

"What a smashing idea, Jim," said Auntie Flo.

"Far be it for me to cast a damper on the proceedings," said Emily Hollins, "but I was looking forward to a weekend's holiday – I don't want to go home and spend the next two days in the kitchen. Besides, I don't know what I'm going to give you all to eat."

"Do you happen to like shrubel-cake?" asked a small voice, tentatively, from the dark of the auditorium.

Switching on the torch again, Henry flashed the beam around the stalls. After some moments, Karl

Gustaffe's face was caught in the light, blinking anxiously over the back of Row D, where he had been in hiding since making his exit from the dressing-room, to escape the fire officer's wrath.

"Aren't you one of the vampire hunters?" asked Henry Hollins.

"I used to be," admitted Gustaffe. "But not by choice. I'm a baker by profession. My vampire hunting job was all Alphonse Kropotel's doing. Now that he's gone, I'd much rather bake shrubel-cakes than hunt vampires."

"He did speak up on my behalf, when the others wanted to hammer a stake in me," said Albert Hollins.

"He makes very good shrubel-cakes too," said the count. "I can vouch for that – I've often tasted his handiwork."

"I'll willingly cook for all of you, for as long as you like, if you'll let me," said the little baker eagerly. "I'd like to. I feel that it's the very least that I can do to make amends."

"What ingredients do you need to make shrubel-cake?" asked Emily Hollins, attracted by the idea of having a Transylvanian cook at her beck and call. It would certainly give the neighbours something to think about.

"Well, goose eggs, for a start," began the little baker, ticking off the items on his fingers. "Then I shall want the root of the zygveny plant which flourishes on the lower slopes of the Tolokovin mountain; next, I shall require some rancid sour cream – "

"I'm not sure that I shall have *exactly* what you

need in my larder," Emily Hollins broke in, hastily. "But I'm sure that I'll be able to find you something that you can use instead."

"It's Saint Unfortunato's Day tomorrow," said Count Alucard, as the fact suddenly occurred to him. "And we shall have shrubel-cakes for tea."

"Brilliant," said Henry Hollins.

THE END (Almost)

UPDATE:

Sergeant-Alphonse Kropotel is back in charge of the Tolokovin police-force. *Karl Gustaffe* is also back in Tolokovin and hard at work in his bakery. Apart from passing the time of day, the two men seldom speak to each other.

Uncle Jim and *Auntie Flo* have left Wolverhampton and now live in Newcastle. They recently won the runners-up trophy in the Northern Counties Mixed Doubles Carpet Bowls Championships. The silver cup, with their names engraved on it, now graces the sideboard in their living-room.

Captain Ozzie Cummings has left the SAS and is currently living in a tent on an island in the Outer Hebrides, where he is writing a book about his military adventures. He is not intending to include the story of his encounter with Count Alucard in his memoirs.

Chief Inspector Arnold Corcoran has retired from the police force, and has bought a little cliff-top café in Scarcombe with his pension. *Detective Constable Kevin Thoroughgood* has also left the police force, but is still working for his old boss, as a chef. His speciality is Baked-Beans-On-Toast.

The Harcourt Hetherington Players have gone from strength to strength. They are currently on tour in the Far East with a production of *A Christmas Carol. Harcourt Hetherington*'s performance as Scrooge is receiving rave reviews. *Colin Lightfoot*, having decided that he was not cut out to be a customs man, has become an actor. He is currently playing Bob Cratchitt in the same production.

Count Alucard is back in residence at Alucard Castle. He is rarely troubled, these days, by the people of Tolokovin, who have wisely decided to live and let live. The Hollinses are frequent visitors at the castle. Whenever she goes to Transylvania, *Emily Hollins* includes several bright yellow dusters in her luggage, for use in her continuing war with the castle's cobwebs.

Albert Hollins makes sure to take along several garden gnomes, which he is introducing, one by one and deeper and deeper, into the forest. *Henry Hollins* never forgets to tuck a couple of packets of dog-biscuits inside his suitcase, as titbits for Count Alucard's children of the night – the wolves of Tolokovin.

The Hollins' cat, *Tibbles* (not previously referred to in these pages), sleeps on a cat-blanket in the sitting-room at 42, Nicholas Nickleby Close, Staplewood, and never ventures outdoors at night.

Sometimes, when Henry Hollins has been kind enough to open the coffin-lid, Tibbles snoozes all through the hours of darkness inside Count Alucard's second-best coffin. Count Alucard has no objection to this arrangement – provided, of course, he is not visiting Staplewood, for a change of air, and sleeping in his coffin himself.

Other great reads *from* **Red Fox**

Whatever you like to read, Red Fox has got the story for you. Why not choose another book from our range of Animal Stories, Funny Stories or Fantastic Stories? Reading has never been so much fun!

Red Fox Funny Stories

THANKS FOR THE SARDINE
Laura Beaumont

Poor Aggie is sick and tired of hearing her mates jabbering on about how brilliant their Aunties are. Aggie's aunties are useless. In fact they're not just boring – they don't even try! Could a spell at Aunt Augusta's Academy of Advanced Auntiness be the answer?

Chucklesome stuff!
Young Telegraph

GIZZMO LEWIS: FAIRLY SECRET AGENT
Michael Coleman

Gizzmo Lewis, newly qualified secret agent from the planet Sigma-6, is on a mission. He's been sent to check out the defences of a nasty little planet full of ugly creatures – yep, you guessed it, he's on planet Earth! It's all a shock to Gizzmo's system so he decides to sort things out – alien-style!

0 09 926631 8 £2.99

THE HOUSE THAT SAILED AWAY
Pat Hutchins

It has rained all holiday! But just as everyone is getting really fed up of being stuck indoors, the house starts to shudder and rock, and then just floats off down the street to the sea. Hungry cannibals, bloody-thirsty pirates and a cunning kidnapping are just some of the hair-raisers in store.

0 09 993200 8 £2.99

Red Fox Fantastic Stories

THE STEALING OF QUEEN VICTORIA
Shirley Isherwood
Boo and his grandmother live above Mr Timms' antique shop. Neither of them has paid too much attention to the old bust of Queen Victoria which sits in the shop – until a strange man offers them some money to steal it for him!
Compelling reading
Book for Keeps
0 09 940152 5 £2.99

THE INFLATABLE SHOP
Willis Hall
The Hollins family is off on holiday– to crummy Cockleton-on-Sea. Some holiday! So one particularly windy, rainy day, it's Henry Hollins' good luck that he steps into Samuel Swain's Inflatable Shop just as a great inflatable adventure is about to begin!
Highly entertaining
Junior Education
0 09 940162 2 £2.99

TRIV IN PURSUIT
Michael Coleman
Something very fishy is happening at St Ethelred's School. One by one all the teachers are vanishing into thin air leaving very odd notes behind. Triv suspects something dodgy is happening. The search is on to solve the mind-boggling mystery of the missing teachers.
0 09 940083 9 £2.99

AGENT Z GOES WILD
Mark Haddon
When Ben sets off on an outward bound trip with Barney and Jenks, he should have realised there'd be crime-busting, top-secret snooping and toothpaste-sabotaging to be done . . .
0 09 940073 1 £2.99

Other great reads from **Red Fox**

Red Fox Animal Stories

FOWL PEST
(Shortlisted for the Smarties Prize)
James Andrew Hall
Amy Pickett wants to be a chicken! Seriously! Understandably her family aren't too keen on the idea. Even Amy's best friend, Clarice, thinks she's unhinged. Then Madam Marvel comes to town and strange feathery things begin to happen.
A Fantastic tale, full of jokes
Child Education
0 09 940182 7 £2.99

OMELETTE: A CHICKEN IN PERIL
Gareth Owen
As the egg breaks, a young chicken pops his head out of the crack to see, with horror, an enormous frying pan. And so Omelette is born into the world! This is just the beginning of a hazardous life for the wide-eyed chicken who must learn to keep his wits about him.
0 09 940013 8 £2.99

ESCAPE TO THE WILD
Colin Dann
Eric made up his mind. He would go to the pet shop, open the cages and let the little troupe of animals escape to the wild.
Readers will find the book unputdownable
Growing Point
0 09 940063 4 £2.99

SEAL SECRET
Aidan Chambers
William is really fed up on holliday in Wales until Gwyn, the boy from the nearby farm, shows him the seal lying in a cave. Gwyn knows exactly what he is going to do with it; William knows he has to stop him . . .
0 09 991500 £2.99

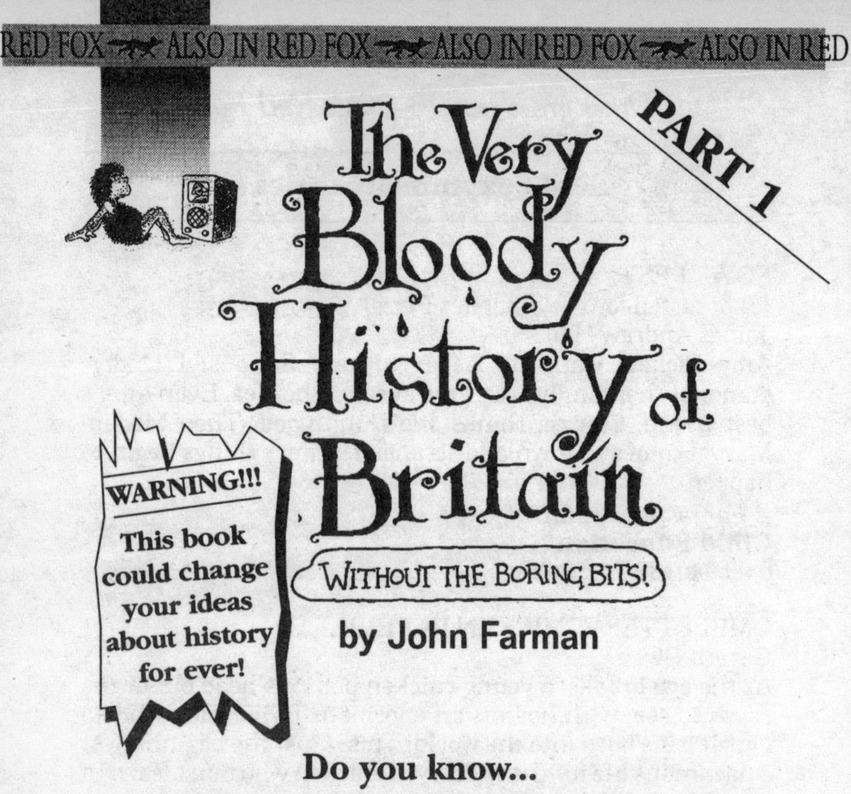

Do you know...

WHO planned the first Channel tunnel?
WHEN 10 Downing Street was built?
WHO invented the television?
WHEN the first Cheddar cheese was made?

Get the low down on life from the heathens to Hitler! Bizarre, barmy and almost beyond belief, John Farman's **THE VERY BLOODY HISTORY** makes boring history lessons a thing of the - er - past.

John Farman
THE VERY BLOODY HISTORY OF BRITAIN PART 1
Red Fox *paperback*, £3.99 ISBN 0 09 984010 3